TEMPTING THE VISCOUNT

LANDING A LORD

SUZANNA MEDEIROS

TEMPTING THE VISCOUNT

She's looking for a lover, but he intends to make her his wife…

After surviving an unhappy marriage, the Dowager Baroness Mansfield plans to enjoy her freedom. But when Lucy meets Viscount Holbrook, she can't ignore the spark of attraction that flares to life between them.

So she does the only logical thing for a woman in her position—she asks him to be her lover. But her unsatisfactory experience with her first husband has her wondering if she's even capable of enjoying such an arrangement.

Holbrook counters by proposing a wager. If he can show her she's capable of experiencing pleasure, she'll allow him to court her.

Holbrook is determined to behave honorably, but Lucy tempts him to give in to his baser desires. His only recourse is to convince her they can both get what they want.

TEMPTING THE VISCOUNT is the final book in Suzanna Medeiros's Landing a Lord series!

To learn about Suzanna Medeiros's future books, you can sign up for her newsletter at www.suzannamedeiros.com/newsletter.

To every one of you who has been along on this incredible journey.

Thank you.

CHAPTER 1

April 1819

One hour. That was how long it took Lucy, the widowed Lady Mansfield, to become uncomfortable with her surroundings.

It wasn't the event exactly. A dinner with her brother, the Duke of Clarington, and his wife Charlotte, who was also her closest friend. But the intimate dinner party the Claringtons held annually on the evening before their ball had increased in size since the last time she'd attended, two years ago.

Lucy had remained in the country last year after her husband of eleven years died. Looking back, she supposed his death had been inevitable. It was only a matter of time before he'd be challenged to a duel by one of the many men he'd cuckolded over the years.

She'd avoided London because she couldn't face the scandal that had swept through the ton after gossip about the duel had spread. Her humiliation had been sufficient without having to deal with the pitying looks and whispers from everyone she knew.

She'd married for love after her first season. But that love quickly turned to hate when the man who'd wooed her relentlessly tired of her company after just one year of marriage.

The pain that overwhelmed her when she first discovered his infidelity faded over the years. Of course her husband had blamed her when she'd failed to bear him an heir. Or any child.

Mansfield had been angry, and he'd thrown his affairs in her face, telling her that if she couldn't give him children, perhaps another woman would. It had been a move calculated to cause her pain, something at which her husband seemed to excel. But when he failed to father even one bastard—despite his diligent efforts to do just that over the years—he'd finally stopped berating her for her inability to fall pregnant.

She'd stayed out of his way, and he'd left her alone.

Lucy didn't miss her husband. The man with whom she'd fallen in love had been a fiction. When her husband died, she realized she'd already mourned the passing of the man she loved many years ago.

She settled more comfortably into an armchair in a corner of her brother's luxuriously appointed drawing room and observed all the guests. Aside from herself, every person present was happily married.

She didn't begrudge them their bliss. But watching the way each couple gazed at their spouse with affection, if not barely concealed adoration, made her feel anxious. And with every loving smile and touch she witnessed, Lucy grew increasingly uncomfortable.

She couldn't help but wonder if something was wrong with her. Why had her love match turned horribly wrong while these people were able to secure happily-ever-afters? It was impossible to believe that true love didn't exist when surrounded by such evidence to the contrary. Apparently love *did* exist. Just not for her.

She dreaded the dinner that would be starting soon. If her sister-in-law hadn't been her closest friend since childhood, Lucy would have pleaded a headache to escape the suffocating bliss. Since she was staying with Alex and Charlotte during the season, it would be easy to slip upstairs and seek solace in her bedchamber.

But Charlotte would know she was lying.

So Lucy smiled and engaged in small talk with the other guests. Above all, she tried to ignore the sensation that she didn't belong with these people. Dinner had yet to be served, and a very real headache was beginning to form, but she ignored it.

And then *he* walked into the room.

Viscount Holbrook.

She'd met the man only briefly before tonight. He was tall with dark brown hair that was kept fashionably short, and his eyes were a deep blue that seemed unnatural.

It was almost unfair how handsome she found him, and in another lifetime she would have gone out of her way to seek his attention. But experience had taught her such men would never be faithful.

She watched as he made his way around the room, greeting all the guests as though they were lifelong friends. She couldn't help but wonder how he'd made it into her brother's inner circle. And watching the way Alex greeted him warmly, it was evident her brother liked him a great deal more than he'd ever liked Lucy's husband.

In the beginning, Alex had tolerated Mansfield because Lucy loved him. After that first year, when it became clear that her husband was intent on bedding every willing woman of the ton, Alex's indifference to Mansfield had turned to something much darker. Her brother wouldn't welcome someone else into their group who behaved in a similar manner.

Perhaps Holbrook limited his love affairs to widows.

A zing of awareness went through her at the thought. She was a widow. There was nothing to stop her from also taking a lover. She might not have love, but that didn't mean she couldn't find enjoyment with a man. Or many.

Distaste soured her mood at that last thought. No, not many men. But perhaps one man. This man. If she could find the courage within herself.

She rose to her feet when he made his way over to where she was sitting.

"Lady Mansfield." He took the hand she held out to him and bowed over it. "It is a pleasure to see you here tonight."

He was too polite to say anything about her

husband—had he known Mansfield?—but his cautious expression made it clear he was curious. He probably assumed she was still mourning his death.

She clasped her hands at her waist as she replied, but she couldn't remember what she said because all her thoughts were centered on the fact that her hand was tingling from where he'd held it.

Neither of them wore gloves. She'd known they wouldn't be necessary since this wasn't a formal dinner, but it surprised her that Holbrook had also foregone wearing them. Just how well did he know her brother?

It was foolish to wonder. If she was considering the possibility of taking a lover, surely she could ask the man a simple question. Not that she believed she'd ever be quite so bold, but it was fun to entertain the notion.

"When my sister-in-law spoke about tonight's dinner party, I wasn't expecting quite so many people to be in attendance." She wanted to wince after the words were out. Had that sounded like an insult? Did he think she was questioning why he'd received an invitation? "I mean no offense, of course. But with the ball tomorrow, I'd assumed there would only be a few people here."

The Marquess of Overlea and the Earl of Kerrick were Alex's closest friends, and they saw each other every day when they were in town. She'd known the two men and their wives would be here tonight, but she hadn't expected everyone else.

The Marquess of Lowenbrock was the brother of Overlea's and Kerrick's wives, so his presence wasn't a surprise. But Viscount Ashford's, Baron Cranston's, and the Earl of Hargrove's attendance was unexpected, as was Holbrook's.

The corners of Holbrook's eyes crinkled as he smiled down at her. "I think Hargrove and Cranston might have lobbied for my presence tonight."

She released the breath she'd been holding. Her husband would have bristled at her words even though no offense had been intended. Clearly Holbrook was more even-tempered. It was yet another point in the man's favor.

"And Charlotte would have agreed because it meant there wouldn't be an uneven number of people at the dinner table."

"It seems that is my role now. The man you invite to your dinner parties to even out the number of guests." Despite his attempt to appear chagrined, he couldn't hide his amusement.

"Well, I for one am glad I won't be the only unmarried person here." She wasn't sure what made her rush to add, "Fear not, I doubt they're matchmaking. Charlotte doesn't think I'm ready for that yet."

His gaze became serious, and she had the uncanny sensation that he saw right through her. Could he sense how broken and uncertain she was beneath the detached demeanor she'd perfected after her husband made her an object of pity?

"Would she be correct in that assumption? That you're not yet ready to…?"

His words trailed off as though he'd only just realized the question was too forward, and her imagination leaped to fill in the blanks. To find love again? To marry? To have a torrid love affair?

She was no innocent. As a widow now out of mourning, she knew men would seek her out. They would issue all manner of lewd invitations—over the years she'd seen it firsthand with other widows, who made no secret of the fact they were enjoying their newfound freedom. But somehow she didn't think that had been Holbrook's intention.

He stiffened as though just realizing what he'd implied, and she laughed when he passed a hand over his face. When he dropped his arm again, his smile was tilted at one corner. The hint of color high on his cheekbones charmed her.

"One would think I'd never spoken to a beautiful woman before. I meant no disrespect, of course. Please don't tell your brother. I'm quite famished and don't relish being thrown out." He leaned in close. "And my friends would retell the tale for the next year for their own entertainment."

She laughed again, amused. She liked the viscount, and she didn't know what to do with that knowledge. "Your secret is safe with me. For now."

The butler stepped into the room then and announced that dinner was ready. Holbrook raised a brow and held out his arm. He'd been invited to act as her dinner partner, so she shouldn't have felt the flutter of nerves low in her belly as she tucked her hand into his elbow.

"I'll endeavor to be on my best behavior for the rest of the night." The rumble of his voice settled over her, low and intimate.

She didn't reply, but she couldn't help the small twinge of disappointment. *But we were just beginning to have so much fun.*

CHAPTER 2

*H*olbrook found it decidedly less enjoyable to attend a ball when every one of his friends was already married. This season he wasn't the sage friend who saw a little too much—and who did what he could to nudge a friend in the right romantic direction. No, this year he was the only bachelor in the group. He was beginning to feel like he didn't quite belong. It wasn't because of anything they said or did, but he couldn't shake the feeling.

It might be time to give serious consideration to settling down. After all, he wasn't exactly cutting a swath through the available women of the ton. If that was what he wanted, he knew he'd be able to find a willing bed partner easily enough. Several women that evening had already dropped discreet hints that they'd be open to a liaison.

But surrounded by his happily married friends, he couldn't ignore the uncomfortable yearning to find the same thing for himself. A woman worthy of his love. One who completed him.

It was a silly, romantic notion, but he'd always been something of a romantic. And yesterday's dinner had shown him that happiness and long-lasting love *was* possible.

It took a great deal of effort to keep from frowning as he scanned the guests who filled the glittering ballroom. He stood off to one side and took in the couples who were already dancing. The women wore brightly colored gowns to showcase their attributes, and while many were smiling, it was clear that an equal number were merely tolerating their partners.

And then there were the young women who were standing with their friends and mamas along the edges of the room, trying to appear as though they weren't desperate to procure their own dance partners.

He didn't know any of them. He imagined the task ahead as he searched for a bride. He'd need to ask many, perhaps even all, of them to dance. Afterward, courtesy dictated that he call on them the next day.

The season stretched ahead of him, a potentially unending series of tedious days and evenings of getting to know them better. Of trying to weed through the silly young chits to find the one woman who would capture his heart. He was already tired just from thinking about it.

He allowed his gaze to move from group to group as he tried to formulate a plan of attack.

Had there always been so many debutantes? Perhaps he should start with the women who were on their second or third seasons. Or maybe he should start with the older group of women sitting off to one side, content to chatter among themselves because they'd ceased their search for a husband. Surely they'd be less likely to talk incessantly about gown colors and hair ribbons.

In all fairness, that had only been one young woman, but she was the only person he'd danced with that evening. Her constant chatter about whether she should have worn a different color gown had tempted him to give up and go home the moment he'd escorted her back to her overeager mother. The older woman had looked him over as though she was already imagining the day he'd return to beg for her daughter's hand in marriage.

"Looking for someone in particular?"

He turned to find Hargrove and his countess of less than a year standing next to him. He hadn't even heard their approach. "Do you have any suggestions? Why are there so many of them this year?"

Lady Hargrove laughed. "There are no more young women here than last year. And I don't recall you behaving so out of sorts then."

"Indeed," Hargrove continued. "Was there anyone you didn't dance with last season? Why are you standing off to the side, scowling at everyone now?"

Holbrook could hardly admit that last year he hadn't cared about finding a wife, so it hadn't taken any effort to enjoy the various balls they'd attended. But now that he'd made up his mind that he wanted what Hargrove had found with Eleanor, he was suddenly at a loss. He had no idea how to go about finding a bride. All the interesting women of his acquaintance were already married.

Or widowed. His thoughts went back to Lady Mansfield. As the only two unmarried people in attendance at last night's dinner party, they'd sat next to each other during the meal, and he'd enjoyed her company very much. She'd even forgiven his horrible gaffe early in the evening when he'd inadvertently propositioned her.

The widow was still a young woman. If she was older than his own age of thirty, it wasn't by much. And she was undeniably beautiful with her dark hair and light blue eyes. He'd found her attractive, of course. Any man would.

But despite her friendly demeanor last night, she'd held herself aloof. More than once he'd seen her eyes glaze over as though she was remembering something. Usually after she witnessed another guest's loving interaction with their spouse.

He couldn't help but wonder if her marriage had been a happy one. He'd heard the rumors, of course. That Mansfield had died after dueling with a man he'd cuckolded. If Lady Mansfield hadn't been aware of his infidelity, the scandal that followed would have devastated her.

No, he couldn't consider her. She was only just out of mourning, and given the way her husband had died, he doubted she was looking for another husband. And being under the protection of her brother, the Duke of Clarington, she wouldn't need to marry again so soon. If ever.

Before he could consider why that thought left him feeling unsettled, she joined their group. It was as though he'd conjured her presence merely by thinking about her.

Lady Hargrove enveloped her in a hug. It was an effusive welcome for such a formal event, and he expected the widow to pull away. Instead, she returned it with equal enthusiasm.

Interesting.

Hargrove bowed his greeting, and when Lady Mansfield turned to him, Holbrook did the same.

Eleanor tucked her arm into Lady Mansfield's, and the pair moved away a short distance, their heads bowed together as they chatted about something. Holbrook wondered what they were discussing that couldn't be said in his presence, but the music and low hum of conversation that surrounded them was enough to keep their whispers private.

Holbrook was powerless to stop his gaze from sweeping down the widow's figure. Her gown was a rich, deep blue. Together with her dark hair, it made her skin appear almost translucent. He wouldn't be a man if he didn't also appreciate the way her low-cut décolletage left a great deal of that skin on display.

Hargrove cleared his throat then, drawing his attention. The gleam in his eyes told Holbrook his friend had noticed where his attention had drifted.

Hargrove raised one brow. "Do you think she'd be interested in marrying again?"

It was unnerving the way the man had read his thoughts. "Doubtful."

"She's a widow," Hargrove said, his expression carefully neutral. "Perhaps she'd be interested in a different sort of arrangement."

Holbrook resisted the urge to reach for his cravat to loosen the fabric that now threatened to strangle him. "Even if she was willing, I don't think it's wise. She's on friendly terms with all the same people I know. It might be inconvenient afterward."

"And of course there's also her brother."

Yes, the Duke of Clarington could make Holbrook's life a living hell for daring to even think about engaging in an affair with his sister. The way the man had hovered near her during their dinner party last night, going out of his way to include her in his conversations with the various guests, made it clear he was very protective of her. And after dinner, when they'd joined the women again in the drawing room, Lady Mansfield hadn't left the duchess's side.

His gaze returned to Eleanor and the widowed baroness. Their dark heads bowed close together, giving the appearance that they were in their own world. Both women were beautiful, but it was Lady Mansfield who held his attention.

He couldn't deny the fact she intrigued him. If she were anyone else, he might have taken Hargrove up on his suggestion and pursued the woman. But she was too enmeshed within his circle. If things ended badly between them…

No, even if everything went smoothly, he couldn't risk Clarington's displeasure. If the duke found out, he'd probably believe Holbrook was taking advantage of his sister.

As if sensing his scrutiny, Lady Mansfield met his gaze. She smiled at him before turning her attention back to Eleanor.

He didn't realize he'd returned the smile until Hargrove bumped shoulders with him. "Careful, old boy. I think you're starting to drool. You don't want the duke to see it."

Holbrook shook his head. "You'll never forgive me for giving you such a hard time last year about Eleanor, will you?"

"On the contrary," Hargrove said. "If you hadn't talked sense into me, I might have lost her."

"I doubt that. I just wish I'd been at Hyde Park to see you make your public declaration of love. It was all anyone could talk about for weeks."

Hargrove grinned and lifted one shoulder in a shrug. "It was worth the momentary embarrassment."

Damn. It appeared that love had rendered his friend impervious to mocking.

CHAPTER 3

ucy found it difficult to concentrate on what Eleanor was saying when her full attention was on Viscount Holbrook. At least her new friend was too sensible to whisk her away from the men just so they could critique what everyone was wearing. It was a topic of conversation Lucy knew would be on many lips at that very moment.

But she'd never enjoyed the act of tearing other women down just to make herself feel better even though she knew many of tonight's guests had taken joy in gossiping about her husband's infidelities. For all she knew, they were talking about her right now. *There she is. I can't believe she has the temerity to show her face. Did you hear about how her husband died?*

Lucy pushed aside those thoughts and concentrated on what Eleanor was saying about a new author she'd recently discovered. When the Countess of Hargrove had learned that Lucy enjoyed reading novels, they'd become instant friends.

The strains of a waltz began to play. As if they'd choreographed it, Eleanor turned to her right just as her husband reached her side. He held out his arm, and Eleanor took it with a besotted smile.

"I hope you don't mind my abandoning you for a few minutes," Eleanor said.

Lucy refused to acknowledge the pang of longing that hit her when she witnessed the intimate way Hargrove looked at his wife. She'd need to grow a thicker skin since she was now surrounded by happily married couples. "Of course not," she murmured, trying to infuse as much warmth as she could into her smile.

She hadn't realized Holbrook was standing off to one side until he spoke.

"I hope you haven't already promised this dance to another?"

His words were polite, but they both knew she hadn't. As a widow, she didn't need to carry a dance card. Men weren't flocking around her for dances.

Not public ones at any rate. No, what they wanted from her was what all men seemed to want from widows. A quick tumble. Widows who hadn't been able to give their husbands children weren't sought after as marriage candidates, but they were very desirable to men who wanted to bed a woman without needing to worry about siring a bastard.

Her brother's warning about that fact last month, when she'd told him she was ready to start attending social events again, had surprised her. But she was glad he'd told her what to expect. It explained why so many men were looking at her. She wondered how long it would be before she received her first proposition.

Her first *real* proposition anyway. Holbrook's embarrassment the previous evening when he realized how she might have interpreted his unfinished statement had amused her.

Her smile was genuine when she took his arm and allowed him to lead her to the center of the ballroom. It was silly, but in that moment she almost felt like the innocent young woman she'd once been, thrilled that a handsome man had asked her to dance. But she couldn't deny that her partner was attracting no small amount of attention from other women.

He kept a circumspect distance between them when she moved into his arms. On the one hand, it meant he wasn't like all the other men who were prowling around the room, waiting for their opportunity to approach her. She could almost feel their eyes on her right now. But here, among all the other couples who were intent only on their dance partner, she could breathe a little easier. No one would be approaching her for the next few minutes.

Still, she couldn't deny that she felt a twinge of sadness at the fact Holbrook would never see her as the hopeful young woman, filled with joy, she'd once been.

Holbrook more than made up for her temporary melancholy with his flair for dancing. He seemed to take a great deal of pleasure in sweeping her across the entire dance floor. When he spun her away from him, then back into his arms, she couldn't hold back her laughter.

"You are quite good at waltzing, my lord."

His grin was wide. "It isn't often that I find a dance partner who can keep up with me."

She searched his expression, looking for any hint of a double entendre. The fact that his words seemed sincere caused a contrary part of her to want to tease him.

She lowered her voice and inched a tiny fraction closer. "I'm happy to hear that. It's not often that I find a *partner* who challenges me."

Lucy wanted to laugh when his eyes widened, then narrowed. He was trying to decide whether he'd read too much into her words. She was enjoying his confusion. And if she was being completely honest, found herself wanting to get to know the viscount better.

Instead of replying, he swept her around the ballroom dance floor again. His movements were confident, and she suspected a less experienced partner would have bumped into at least one other couple. But somehow Holbrook managed the feat even though he spent most of that time looking down at her.

When the music finally drew to a close, she was much too close to him. His stare bored straight through to her soul, and she was very aware of the way her breath was coming out in small pants.

They stayed that way for what seemed an eternity. Surely much longer than was appropriate. The spell was broken, however, when someone clapped Holbrook on the shoulder.

She was only peripherally aware of the man who'd interrupted. He asked her for the next dance

—not a waltz thankfully. She accepted with a small nod and allowed him to lead her to join one of the sets that was forming.

She turned back once, some instinct telling her exactly where to look. Holbrook had moved off to the side of the room and was leaning casually against the wall. Two young women walked in front of him, slowing as they passed, hoping he would notice them and ask one of them to dance. But his gaze remained fixed on her.

When Lucy turned back to her partner, it took a great deal of effort to hold back her grin.

Later, when that dance was over, she couldn't remember whom she'd danced with, nor did she care. A plan—a crazy, insane plan—was beginning to take shape.

CHAPTER 4

*H*er unhappy marriage had taught Lucy a valuable lesson. Never again would she rush into a romantic relationship. After her brother and her best friend had fallen in love and married, she'd been convinced that Mansfield would be her own happily-ever-after.

She couldn't have been more wrong. But the fact she wasn't looking for love didn't mean she couldn't explore another physical relationship with a man.

Anticipation filled her entire being as she considered exploring such intimacies with Holbrook. It was beyond impulsive. She'd just escaped a loveless marriage that had convinced her she was physically incapable of experiencing pleasure with a man. She never had with her husband, not even during those first few months of her marriage when she'd still loved him.

She was a widow now and free to do whatever she wanted. She could take a lover. But she wasn't sure it was wise to consider the first man to whom she now felt an attraction. She'd done that at eighteen, when she was newly out in society. She wouldn't make that mistake a second time.

So she avoided Holbrook for the rest of the ball. Before she could move forward with her plans, she needed to discover whether she could experience a similar attraction to another man. It would be easier, after all, to conduct a discreet affair with someone who wasn't a close acquaintance of her brother.

For the next few hours, she spoke to the men who sought her company and danced with those who asked her. She was careful, however, not to be alone with them.

Despite her determination to keep an open mind, she felt no spark of attraction for any of those men. And for some reason, she could still feel Holbrook's gaze on her. She was careful not to be caught staring at the man, but a discreet peek here and there told her she wasn't imagining things.

Even when he was dancing with other women, Holbrook kept glancing her way.

And every time their eyes met, a thrill of anticipation surged through her.

Several hours passed that way, and Lucy's feet were starting to ache from the unaccustomed exercise. She'd been a young woman of eighteen, newly out in society, the last time she'd danced this much in one evening. At thirty-one, she would hardly be considered old, but it seemed that her endurance had finally reached its limits.

She rejoined Charlotte and her brother, who were also returning from their most recent dance. She didn't miss the significant look her friend cast her husband before she turned to Lucy and linked arms with her.

"Let's get something to drink," Charlotte said.

Lucy should have realized her friend had an ulterior motive, but she was so distracted by her own musings she didn't notice when Charlotte walked past the refreshment tables.

They were in the hallway before Lucy realized they'd left the ballroom. Assuming Charlotte needed the retiring room, she turned left, but her friend tugged her in the opposite direction.

They passed several footmen along the way, but

Charlotte kept walking. When they reached the library, she led them into the room.

Bemused, Lucy waited for her friend to close the door before speaking. "What could have happened to cause you to leave the ball just so you could speak to me? I'm sure that whatever it was could have waited until tomorrow."

Charlotte placed her hands on her hips and examined her for several seconds before speaking. "Is something happening between you and Lord Holbrook?"

Lucy froze at the question and then let out a soft sigh. She'd wanted to discuss this very subject with her friend tomorrow. But Charlotte knew her well, so it was inevitable she'd noticed Lucy's interest in the man.

"Am I so obvious?" Lucy dropped onto the settee that was tucked into one corner of the room.

Several such seating arrangements were scattered throughout the large library amid the many bookshelves, making it one of Lucy's favorite places in her brother's town house. It seemed it would also be the room where Lucy was going to confess her scandalous plans.

Charlotte grinned and settled next to her. "Only to me. The two of you got along well last night.

Then there was that waltz." She fanned herself in an exaggerated manner.

Lucy frowned. "It was just a waltz."

Charlotte made a soft tsking sound. "After which the two of you have been sneaking glances at each other all night."

Lucy groaned. "I thought I was being subtle."

"You were. But he wasn't pleased about the fact that you've danced at least once with every eligible man here."

Lucy felt a little thrill at her friend's confirmation that she hadn't been imagining things. She'd half worried she was seeing only what she wanted to see. "How well do you know him?"

"We've met a few times and I like him, but Alex sees him often. And you know he wouldn't have invited him to dinner last night if he didn't think highly of him."

She couldn't hold back a small smile at Charlotte's attempt to appear nonchalant. "You're matchmaking."

Charlotte reached for one of her hands and gave it a quick squeeze. "Please don't be angry. Alex and I are only together because of your assistance. I want to see you happy as well."

Lucy sighed. "After my marriage, I'm not sure that's possible."

She hated the sad look on Charlotte's face.

"Not every man is like Mansfield," Charlotte said. "Alex's friends, the other men who were here last night... They're all happily married. And faithful to their wives."

Lucy found it difficult to hold back her discomfort with this subject. It wasn't as though Charlotte hadn't been aware of Lucy's husband's infidelities, but they'd never spoken about it openly.

Lucy didn't want to dwell on the past. "I have no plans to marry again. But..." She had to take another deep breath before she could continue. It was impossible to believe she was actually considering this. "But there's no reason I can't take a lover."

Charlotte's mouth dropped open. Her expression of shock was so comical Lucy would have laughed if her own heart wasn't racing.

"Holbrook?" Charlotte's voice was barely above a whisper.

Lucy nodded. "There's no one holding me back now."

They both knew she could have had an affair while married. Heaven knew her husband had left her alone for long periods of time. Lucy had even considered it on several occasions. But even if she'd been tempted—and she'd never met a man before now who would have made her consider it—she'd meant her wedding vows. Even after she'd grown to despise the man she'd married, she would never go back on her sacred promise to remain faithful to him.

Lucy could almost see the wheels turning in her friend's mind. It was a great relief that Charlotte hadn't rushed to talk her out of her plan. Still, she needed her friend's reassurance and so she asked, "Do you think he'd consider it?"

Charlotte's smile was instantaneous. "Oh, he'll definitely be interested. But it remains to be seen if he's willing to risk the wrath of the Duke of Clarington."

Relief flooded through Lucy. "I'll have to see what I can do to tempt him."

They both stood, and Charlotte drew her into a hug. "Please let me help you."

And with that, the plan was set in motion.

CHAPTER 5

After waltzing with Lady Mansfield, Holbrook tried to turn his attention to the task of finding a bride. The undertaking wouldn't be easy, but he wouldn't succeed if he allowed himself to become distracted from his mission.

And after their dance, it was obvious she had the potential to be a very large distraction.

That reality was made abundantly clear when he found himself watching her as she flitted from one dance partner to another. And each time another man so much as smiled at her, he grew increasingly irate.

At first he attributed the emotion to annoyance with her brother. Everyone knew exactly why those men were going out of their way to dance with a widow who was newly out in society again. So why was Clarington allowing it?

But as the hours crawled by, he came to the uncomfortable realization that Lady Mansfield was the only woman in the room who'd captured his romantic interest.

It was deuced inconvenient.

He watched as her most recent dance partner bowed to her. Before someone else could demand her attention, she rejoined the duke and duchess. He felt a measure of relief, knowing she'd be in good hands with her brother.

He forced himself to turn away and make another circuit of the room, nodding to acquaintances as he passed. He'd already spoken to anyone worthy of more than a few minutes of his time.

When he approached the exit that led to the other open rooms on this side of the large town house, he considered escaping to the card room. It would be easier on his increasingly agitated nerves if he didn't have to watch the sharks who were circling the duke's sister, looking for an opportunity to approach her again.

The strains of another waltz began to play, and he cursed under his breath. He needed to make sure she wouldn't be forced to dance with someone who was entirely inappropriate, and he wasn't sure he could trust Clarington to guarantee that wouldn't happen. He imagined that several men had already leaped into action, hoping to take advantage of the opportunity the dance would provide to have her in their arms.

He scanned the couples who were making their way to the ballroom's dance floor, looking to secure a private spot for themselves. The men bowed, the women curtsied, and then they moved into each other's arms.

He was aware he was clenching his jaw but couldn't force himself to relax, especially when he couldn't find her. He did see the duke speaking with a group of older men whom Holbrook knew were trying to gain Clarington's support for a bill that was about to be introduced in Parliament.

Where was the duchess? Perhaps Lady Mansfield was with her sister-in-law. If not, someone might have already spirited her away through one of the open garden doors.

He supposed it was possible she'd already retired for the night. He knew she stayed with her brother when she was in town, so she might have gone upstairs.

Dammit, he shouldn't have taken his eyes off

her. He turned toward the garden doors, deter-mined to search the grounds in case Lady Mansfield needed assistance.

"Lord Holbrook."

He wanted to curse, but when he turned and saw it was the duchess who'd sought his attention, he felt a measure of relief. He looked past her, expecting to find Lady Mansfield with her friend. But the duchess was alone.

"Are you looking for someone, my lord?"

The Duchess of Clarington was an imposing figure. Her red hair was styled elaborately, diamonds winking throughout the mass. She wore emeralds at her throat and ears and a dark green gown that accentuated her coloring.

She was quite tall for a woman, and that height should have made her seem aloof. But despite her lofty stature and status in society, the woman was approachable. Unlike other duchesses, who thought themselves superior to those of lower status, Clar-ington's wife was universally liked.

There was a gleam in her eyes, and he realized that somehow the duchess was aware of his interest in her friend. There was no point in hiding it. Besides, every second he delayed here could mean someone was taking advantage of the beautiful widow.

"Have you seen Lady Mansfield? I thought she was with you."

Her eyes narrowed as she examined him. "My sister-in-law has retired for the evening."

Relief swept through him. Thank God.

The duchess lowered her voice. "Ask me to dance, my lord. I wish to speak with you."

The waltz was already underway, but there was nothing to stop them from joining the other couples, something that would have been impossible if the dance had been a quadrille.

He swept into a low bow. "Your Grace, would you do me the honor of dancing with me?"

Her eyes were sparkling as she dipped into a curtsy before taking his arm. She wasted no time in coming right to the reason she wanted to speak to him. "What are your intentions with respect to my sister-in-law?"

That was the question, wasn't it? He didn't know what his intentions were. He only knew that he liked Lady Mansfield a great deal. That he wanted to get to know her better and had an irrational desire to call out every man who'd danced with her that evening.

He decided to turn the question back to her. "Have I been inappropriate in my attentions?"

She let out a soft sigh, and unless he was mistaken, he thought he detected a hint of disappointment. Perhaps his invitation to dinner last night had been a matchmaking attempt after all.

"So you don't feel any romantic attraction to Lady Mansfield?"

Good heavens, this woman was direct. He'd give her the same honesty in response. "I would be lying if I said I didn't find her intriguing. But given how much attention she's received this evening, I don't think I'm alone in that sentiment." He'd tried to keep his voice even, hoping he wouldn't betray his earlier annoyance.

The way the duchess's lips turned up in satisfaction told him he hadn't been successful. "I'm not surprised. She has much to recommend her."

"Lady Mansfield is beautiful—no one here would deny that. But she's also the duke's sister, and I would never presume—"

"You should."

He almost faltered. Instead, he turned the near misstep into an exaggerated sweep, weaving them through a few of the more staid couples who were barely moving.

The duchess's brows rose a fraction. "You are a very good dancer, my lord. That bodes well for other activities."

What was happening here? Surely the duchess wasn't trying to encourage his inappropriate interest in her sister-in-law. "I sincerely hope you're not about to proposition me."

The duchess laughed. "Good heavens, no. I think we both know that wasn't what I meant."

"I'm almost afraid to continue this conversation."

The duchess examined him for several long moments that had him wondering just how long this waltz was going to last.

Finally, just as he'd begun to think she was going to let the matter drop, she spoke again. "Tell me, my lord, is there anyone on whom you've set your sights this season?"

He might as well be honest. It seemed that the duchess was determined to satisfy her curiosity. "Prior to this evening, I would have said no. But now…" He began moving toward the edge of the ballroom dance floor, which was less crowded. "But now there might be someone."

"Lucy? I mean Lady Mansfield?"

There would be no denying it after tonight if he decided to pursue her. "Perhaps."

"Excellent. I'm going to help you." Her satisfaction was clear.

He wanted to groan. For a heartbeat he wondered whether he was actually ready for this. It was one thing to consider searching for a wife but another entirely to commit himself to the task.

But then he remembered all those other men who'd swarmed around Lady Mansfield all evening and realized it didn't really matter whether he was ready. Time was a luxury he didn't have. The one thing he did know with a bone-deep certainty was that he couldn't stand the idea of Lady Mansfield with one of those other men.

"I wasn't aware she was looking to marry again so soon."

The duchess sighed. "She insists she isn't ready to entertain that possibility."

He felt a pang of dismay that surprised him. "So there is no point in continuing this conversation."

Was he actually disappointed that he wouldn't be able to court the duke's sister? Hours ago, he'd told Hargrove that any kind of relationship between them would be complicated since it might lead to him being barred from receiving future invitations that might include the Claringtons. And even if he weren't banned, it could very well make social situations more than a little awkward. But now he found that he didn't want to just know Lady Mansfield better. He actually *wanted* to court her.

"I would like the opportunity to become acquainted with the baroness. But I won't force my attentions on her if she's not looking to marry again." He'd just have to devote his time to keeping the sharks away from her.

The duchess beamed up at him. "You'll need to tempt her to change her mind."

He'd always liked this woman, but now she was fast becoming one of his favorite people. "What did you have in mind?"

"I've known Lucy my whole life, and she can be a little stubborn once she's settled on a course of action. But I have reason to believe she wouldn't mind receiving your attention."

The duchess and Lady Mansfield must have spoken about him. Her Grace was happily married, and the Claringtons were widely considered to be one of the few couples that proved love in marriage could be more than just a fairy tale. Surely the duchess wouldn't be encouraging him in this way, against her friend's stated desire to remain unmarried, if she didn't know that Lady Mansfield also felt the simmering attraction that was brewing between them.

He hadn't thought it was one-sided, but it was gratifying to have his suspicions confirmed.

Somehow he kept from laughing out loud when he thought of all the other men who were preening about, hoping to gain her favor even if only for just one night.

The duchess had made it known she was willing to help him, and he wasn't too proud to accept her assistance. "How do you suggest I proceed?"

"I spoke with Lady Mansfield before she retired for the night. She informed me that she is willing to receive your call tomorrow."

He was so fixated on their conversation that he almost missed the couple that was barreling toward them. A young man and an almost-painfully-young woman who were so occupied with each other that they weren't paying attention to the other couples moving around them.

Holbrook turned the duchess to the left, and the oblivious pair swept past them with only inches to spare. Unfortunately, another couple wasn't quite so fortunate, and there was a huff of indignation and hastily murmured apologies before the young couple moved off at a more sedate pace.

The duchess laughed. "That was a near miss. Who would have thought a waltz could be so hazardous?"

He managed to smile in reply, but his thoughts were already occupied with the next obstacle in his path. "Should I speak with the duke tonight and let him know I'm interested in courting his sister?"

The duchess shook her head. "Good heavens, no. For now it would be best if we don't inform my dear husband about this matter." He was about to protest, but she continued. "Trust me. Call tomorrow afternoon and speak to Lucy first. There are matters the two of you need to discuss before my husband can be made aware of your courtship."

He would have to take her word on the matter, but keeping the duke in the dark didn't sit well with him. It made Holbrook feel as though his interest in Lady Mansfield wasn't honorable. "The duke won't wonder why I'm calling?"

She shook her head. "He has several appointments tomorrow afternoon. Don't worry—I have faith that everything will work out as it should."

CHAPTER 6

When Lucy opened her eyes, her first thought was of her waltz with Lord Holbrook last night. Despite the fact she'd danced with many men afterward, the details of that waltz with the viscount was the only memory that had taken hold of her imagination.

The way he'd looked, tall and handsome, his eyes filled with friendly warmth. And when she closed her eyes and sank into that moment, she could almost feel the weight of his hand at her waist, his other hand lightly holding hers, guiding her with supreme ease and confidence across the dance floor.

His arm where she'd gripped him had been surprisingly firm. Her husband had been slim and he'd taken great pride in his appearance, but there was a very important difference between the two men. Holbrook had muscles that Mansfield hadn't possessed.

She wondered how his chest would feel…

Her eyes snapped open, and she sat up in bed. What was she doing? Last night she'd told Charlotte she was considering having an affair with Lord Holbrook. But in the clear light of day, removed from the romance of last night's ball, she was starting to have second thoughts about that plan.

She wasn't brave. Things that had seemed possible when she'd felt his eyes following her all evening now seemed foolhardy.

When she'd left Charlotte after their discussion in the library, her friend had assured her she would invite Holbrook to call today. Which meant Lucy would have to face the man very soon.

She rang the bell for her maid, and the young woman slipped into her room minutes later. Her mind was a whirl of indecision as she dressed for the day. As her maid helped her into a pale yellow morning gown and pinned up her hair, Lucy forced herself to try to remember all those other men she'd danced with after leaving Holbrook. She hadn't waltzed with anyone else, so there hadn't been an opportunity to engage in deep conversation with another man. But even if she had, it was clear those men weren't interested in conversing with her.

Mainly they'd talked about themselves. And there'd been no subtlety in the way they dropped lewd promises about their prowess in bed whenever the figures of the sets had brought them together. And did they really think to capture her interest by boasting about how many women would love to be the object of their attention?

Every one of them had reminded her of Mansfield. She couldn't help but imagine her husband spouting similar lines to other women. Luring them into dark corners or sneaking into their homes for a quick tumble. As far as she knew, her husband had never kept a mistress, but she wouldn't have been surprised to learn that he had.

Lucy knew it would be hours yet before Charlotte and Alex rose for the day. While she'd been able to retire just before midnight, they'd had to stay until the ball ended many hours later. Today the servants would be busy putting the house to rights again, cleaning and straightening all the rooms that had been open to guests last night. Lucy didn't like adding to their already increased workload that morning, and so she opted for a simple breakfast tray in her room.

As the morning hours passed, her initial doubts after waking began to shift toward anticipation. But that didn't mean she wasn't second-guessing the crazy plan she'd outlined to Charlotte. One moment she was convinced she would have to speak to the man about how there could be nothing more than friendship between them. Then, a few minutes later, she'd convinced herself to pursue her original course of action and propose they have an affair.

If she allowed him to take the lead, would he propose a discreet liaison? She might have to flirt with him to gain that outcome. Or perhaps it would be better if she was the one to raise the subject.

You have many friends and acquaintances in common. He might not want to risk losing those friendships for a quick tumble with you.

She frowned at that intrusive thought. Her husband wouldn't have cared. In fact, he'd taken delight in the knowledge that the great Duke of Clarington had been powerless to prevent his brother-in-law, who was a mere baron, from doing whatever he wanted.

But Mansfield had been mistaken in thinking Alex had left him alone because he didn't care about Mansfield's behavior. Alex would have moved heaven and earth to secure his sister's happiness. He'd even gone so far as to risk the censure of society when he'd told Lucy that he wanted her to divorce the man.

No, Alex had turned a blind eye to Mansfield's not-so-secret indiscretions because Lucy had asked him to. She hadn't spoken to her brother out of a desire to protect her husband but because she no longer cared what he did. Toward the end of their marriage, they'd lived separately and Lucy had enjoyed the measure of freedom she had in never seeing her husband.

And now that she was well and truly free from her disappointing marriage to a man she'd once thought she loved, she would never again risk her heart.

Which is why you should have an affair with Holbrook. Let him know you're not looking for happily ever after. Take the opportunity to experiment with the physical side of love. Learn for yourself if there is something wrong with you.

She couldn't seem to make up her mind what she wanted to do, and she couldn't find anything with which to distract her from her dilemma. Everyone she knew was already in town, so there was no one to whom she could write a letter. Normally Lucy spent most of her time with Charlotte when they were in town together. When Charlotte wasn't off somewhere with her husband, that is, doing whatever it was that happily married couples of thirteen years did. Lucy tried not to think about what her friend and her brother got up to when they were alone together.

It seemed that Charlotte and Alex were never going to rise that morning. She'd been able to spend half an hour with her nieces and nephews, but then they were whisked away by their governess to attend to their lessons.

Feeling wistful after their boisterous voices disappeared into the schoolroom, she made her way to the gardens. They were just beginning to come to life now that spring had arrived. Charlotte found her several hours later in the rose garden. Only one of the bushes was in bloom, but the sight of the pale pink blossoms made Lucy happy.

Charlotte lowered herself onto the garden bench next to her.

"I think this is my favorite part of the house," Lucy said. "Growing up, I never realized how much of a luxury it was to have a London town house with such a large garden." Mansfield's London home had been nicely appointed, but he was one of the majority of people who didn't have a private garden.

Charlotte wrapped an arm around her shoulders and gave her a quick squeeze. "I trust you slept better than me? I feel as though I'd only just fallen asleep when it was time to wake up again."

Lucy brought her hands up to cover her ears. "How many times have I asked you not to share details about your bedroom activities with my brother!"

Charlotte laughed and Lucy dropped her hands, her own mood lightening. "You're terrible," her sister-in-law said. "We aren't that bad. And certainly not after being awake all night!"

Lucy was silent as she tried to decide how to bring up the subject of Holbrook. Fortunately, Charlotte saved her the trouble.

Her friend leaned against her, their shoulders touching. "Lord Holbrook will be calling soon. For what it's worth, I like him a great deal."

Lucy felt a measure of relief. "You never liked Mansfield."

"I never liked him for *you*. But no one is to blame about what happened. He didn't have a reputation for being a rake."

"I should have gotten to know him better. Alex also had reservations about him."

"We were young. I was thrilled you'd found someone as well and wanted to believe the two of you could have the same relationship as Alex and me. And so I pushed aside my misgivings."

Lucy remembered the one conversation they'd had on the subject. Charlotte had asked her if she was certain she wanted to marry Mansfield. There had been something in her friend's tone that Lucy knew meant her friend was worried about their betrothal. But Lucy had been young and foolish and had gone on and on about all the nice things he'd done for her and how he'd proclaimed his love with such fervor.

The truth was she'd *wanted* to believe that she could have what Charlotte had found with Alex. And Mansfield had taken advantage of her naivete.

Lucy turned so she could face her friend. "You don't think I'm being too rash now? I was so certain last night about what I wanted, but now... I'm having second thoughts."

"I think Holbrook is a good man. No one knows what the future holds, but it's normal to be scared. I was, too, when we came up with that crazy scheme to see if we could make Alex fall in love with me."

Lucy laughed, remembering her brother's annoyance when she and Mama had insisted he accompany them to Almack's. And when their mother had urged him to dance with Charlotte, it was a miracle he hadn't slipped out through a window. "He was less than pleased with us, but everything worked out in the end."

"Yes. For what it's worth, I support your decision. I think getting to know Holbrook better will be good for you."

Lucy took a deep breath, preparing to disappoint her friend. "I'm not looking for love."

"No." Charlotte's smile held more than a hint of sadness. "But perhaps you'll find it anyway."

Lucy didn't argue. There was no point, after all. Love wasn't in the cards for her, but that didn't mean she couldn't find a measure of happiness.

A footman approached and stood off to one side. He held out a silver tray upon which rested one item—a white calling card. Charlotte took it, and together they looked at the name.

Viscount Holbrook.

"Thank you," Charlotte said. "We'll join him shortly."

The footman bowed and turned to leave. Lucy waited until he was out of sight before standing.

"Should I go with you to the drawing room? Or perhaps I should go alone." She was filled with indecision again.

Charlotte stood as well and clasped both her hands. "What would be easiest? I can go see him first, and you can join us in a few minutes. Or perhaps I can tell him to join you here in the garden."

Lucy took a few deep breaths and closed her eyes for a moment, weighing the options. An image of Holbrook smiling down at her while they waltzed last night filled her mind. Then one of him standing by the sidelines, his annoyance clear while he watched her dance with another man.

And she realized that the emotion surging through her wasn't fear or anxiety. It was excitement. She couldn't wait to see him again.

"I'll go see him," she said.

Charlotte smiled and gave her a quick hug. Without another word, Lucy made her way into the house.

She was about to proposition a handsome viscount.

When she entered the drawing room, Holbrook was already rising from an armchair. He bowed and greeted her with a smile that tugged at her foolish heart. There was a warmth in his eyes that was almost enough to convince her she was the only woman in the world instead of just the only one here now.

She asked the footman to bring refreshments before moving farther into the room. Her heart was already racing when she lowered herself onto the end of the settee that was closest to his seat.

She clasped her hands together in her lap and tried to appear composed. It was more difficult than she would have imagined. "I'm pleased to see you, my lord. I hope you enjoyed the ball last night."

"I enjoyed the beginning. And our waltz, of course. But I'm afraid my enjoyment plummeted when I had to watch you dancing with every unmarried man in the room."

Good heavens, it appeared she wouldn't need to worry about how to discreetly bring up the subject of having an affair. But it was a relief to know she hadn't imagined his interest in her. He *had* been watching her. It was one thing to have Charlotte say as much, but it carried more weight coming from Holbrook himself.

She couldn't hide her amusement. "I seem to recall a fair number of young women there. And it was impossible to miss the way many of them were going out of their way to gain your attention."

He settled back into the armchair, his eyes focused on her. "There were other women there?"

She laughed. It was the sort of ridiculous flattery other men used, but for some reason she didn't mind it coming from Holbrook.

She took a deep breath in a vain attempt to settle her nerves. Until that moment, she hadn't been certain she was going to go forward with the crazy scheme. But there was something about Holbrook that set every one of her nerve endings on fire. It was a sensation so far outside anything she'd ever experienced, and she felt a bone-deep need to explore it further.

"Thank you for calling today, my lord."

His body was relaxed, but she could tell from the slight narrowing of his eyes that the effort to keep up that appearance cost him. Why hadn't she asked Charlotte for details about what she'd said to him last night?

"I was surprised to receive the invitation from the duchess."

"What did she tell you?"

There was a brief hesitation before he replied, as though he was considering his response. "She asked me about my intentions. She also led me to believe you'd agree to allow me to court you."

Ice settled over her along with a healthy measure of fear. Courtship? Was he actually here to court her? That was the last thing she wanted. She needed to correct his mistake immediately. "I'm not looking for another husband."

"The duchess—"

He stopped when the footman returned with their tea tray, and Lucy was happy for the short reprieve. This was a disaster. She'd been very clear with Charlotte that she wouldn't marry again, so why would Holbrook think that's what she wanted?

Heat suffused her cheeks, but she ignored her embarrassment and asked him how he took his tea before pouring. It was ridiculous that she was more embarrassed by the idea that Holbrook might think she was searching for another husband than her real reason for wanting to see him today.

She handed him his cup, taking care that their ungloved hands wouldn't touch, before pouring her own. The footman had already left, but Holbrook waited for her to finish pouring her own tea before continuing.

"Your sister-in-law did say that."

She closed her eyes with relief. When she opened them again, he was watching her carefully. "So Charlotte didn't invite you here to court me. Thank heavens."

"If you're not looking for a husband, my lady, then why am I here?"

He was going to make her say it. *Any* other man would have already taken advantage of the opportunity provided by being alone with her and propositioned her. But it seemed she was intent on trying to tempt the one man who didn't want to have an affair with her.

She stood and made her way to the door. It occurred to her that she could flee the room, but there was no escaping now. She'd set things in motion last night when she told Charlotte she wanted to have an affair with this man, and that hadn't changed. If she didn't do this now, she might never again muster the courage.

So instead of running away, she closed the door and turned to face him. He'd risen from his chair but hadn't closed the distance between them.

"I thought that, perhaps, you might want to…" The words lodged in her throat, and she was unable to continue. Embarrassment swept through her, and she could feel her cheeks heat.

Slowly he stalked toward her, his gaze intent on her face. If she had an ounce of self-preservation, she would turn and escape. But she wanted this. She wanted *him*. And from the heat in his eyes, it was obvious he now knew why she'd invited him here.

"It seems we are at cross-purposes. I came here looking for a wife, but unless I'm mistaken, you're looking for a lover."

Her mouth was dry, and she had to swallow before she could continue. "Not just any lover. You."

One corner of his mouth tilted up, and she felt

a corresponding smile spread over her face. "Just to be clear, I don't share."

Heat exploded through her. "Neither do I. Never again." Which was why she'd never remarry. Once wedding vows were spoken, her ability to leave would disappear.

"So the only thing you want from me is carnal pleasure?"

Yes, that was exactly what she wanted. But she found herself saying, "I'm not sure I'd use the word *pleasure*."

He frowned. "You doubt my ability to bring you to completion?"

She could feel her cheeks heating. Never had she spoken aloud about lovemaking. She'd participated in the act with her husband, of course, but they'd never actually discussed the subject. Mansfield did what he wanted, and she lay there and allowed him his marital rights. Until she failed to give him a child, that is. After that, he took his pleasure elsewhere.

Yet Charlotte was very happy in her marriage. And from the brief comments she'd dropped into their conversations over the years—despite Lucy's protestations that she disliked hearing about what

Charlotte got up to with her brother—it was very clear that Charlotte enjoyed their lovemaking.

She had to look away before confessing her deepest secret. But if she was hoping for a physical liaison with Holbrook, it was only fair that he knew the truth. "I think there might be something wrong with me."

Silence stretched between them, and she wanted to sink into the floor in mortification. She could just imagine the look on Holbrook's face. He'd be alarmed, perhaps disgusted. Whatever the exact emotion, he'd realize he was wasting his time with her. No doubt he thought she'd driven her husband into the beds of other women.

She expected him to make an excuse and leave. Instead, gentle fingers touched her chin and turned her face to him.

The heat of his fingers on her skin caused a deep yearning to spring to life within her, but she kept her eyes downcast.

The soft brush of his thumb across her lower lip shocked her. Her eyes widened and she stared at him. He didn't stop, his gaze focused on where he was touching her, but when she shivered, one corner of his mouth lifted. She was becoming very fond of that lopsided smile.

"There is nothing wrong with you. I suspect your husband never bothered to show you what was possible between a man and a woman."

She wanted to believe him. To believe that her dislike of the physical act of lovemaking was more a condemnation of Mansfield than a failing on her part.

She certainly liked the way Holbrook was looking at her now and how he was touching her. It was the lightest of caresses, but his touch caused a spark of desire that shocked her.

"Show me." The plea slipped out almost of its own volition, but she wouldn't pull away from him now. It seemed she was physically incapable of denying this man anything.

They stood in shadows, away from the light cast by the tall north-facing windows. His back blocked the waning afternoon light, and as he stared down at her, his eyes appeared almost black. Only the smallest amount of blue was visible.

His hand remained on her chin, lightly holding her in place as she waited, breathless. He lowered his face to hers, and she realized he was giving her time to change her mind. But Lucy wouldn't. She wanted his kiss with a desperation that surprised her. Even when Mansfield had courted her and she thought herself in love with him, she'd never felt this way.

She reached for Holbrook's wrist to hold him in place, intent on ensuring he wouldn't change his mind and pull away.

Heat flared in his eyes, and it seemed that her simple touch was the inducement he needed to bring his mouth to hers.

She expected him to ravage her mouth. It was always that way with her husband. He'd had two types of kisses. The first was a small peck, the lightest brush of his lips on the back of her hand or on her cheek when he was in the presence of friends and family. That was the public act he put on to show the world he was a devoted husband.

But in the private of her bedchamber, he fell on her with open-mouthed kisses that, thankfully, didn't last long before he got on with the business of thrusting into her.

There would be none of the latter now, of course, but Lucy was surprised that she was almost lightheaded with anticipation.

Holbrook's mouth touched hers with a lightness that frustrated her. It seemed he thought her worthy of only the polite type of kiss and he was going to pull away now.

But then his arms snaked around her and pressed her flush against his body.

The suddenness of the action caused her to gasp in surprise, which was all the encouragement Holbrook needed to kiss her in earnest.

Only he didn't plunge his tongue into her mouth. Instead, he traced her lower lip before dipping inside.

Instead of the disgust she'd felt when Mansfield kissed her, heat began to unfurl within her. A desperation to keep him there seized her, their mouths fused together in long, languorous kisses.

"Lucy."

Her name was uttered on a groan, and she very much liked the sound of it on his lips.

She didn't realize she'd speared her fingers into his hair until he lifted his head to stare down at her. His breath was coming in short pants, echoing her own.

Several long moments passed, and she could almost see the battle being waged within him. She was disappointed that this brief interlude was over far too soon.

She tore her gaze from his and lowered her hands to his shoulders. But she didn't release him. It seemed her traitorous body was unwilling to give up the fantasy that this man could give her something her husband never had. The carnal pleasure he'd promised her.

She licked her lips and kept her eyes lowered. "Thank you. That was quite nice." She was proud of the way she'd managed to keep her tone even.

His bark of laughter surprised her, and she looked up at him.

"Does it take so little to make you happy? To fulfill your desires?"

Her cheeks were already warm from their kiss, so at least she wouldn't suffer the indignity of letting him see the way his words embarrassed her.

Refusing to look away, she raised one shoulder in feigned disinterest. "It's been my experience that what comes next holds very little pleasure for the woman."

His brows drew together, and she wondered if she'd revealed too much. Never mind—she was no innocent. He knew she'd experienced what came next many times. There was nothing he could do or say that would shock her.

"Tell me, Lucy, are you one for wagers?"

He was too close, his expression too intense. And she was very aware of the way her body was still pressed against his. His manhood pushed into her abdomen, a telltale sign that he wanted her.

And for some insane reason, she wanted him too. She didn't know why. Whatever was happening between them was doomed to end in disappointment. Still, she couldn't deny that she was intrigued by the possibilities this man presented.

"That would depend on the wager, of course."

He lowered his head, and she thought he was going to kiss her again. A thrill of anticipation went through her. She quite liked his kisses.

Instead, his mouth skimmed across her cheek, stopping when he reached her ear.

"Did your husband ever bring you such mindless pleasure you were screaming out in ecstasy as you writhed in his arms?"

He was trying to unsettle her. Such a thing wasn't possible.

Or at least it wasn't possible for her. Still, his words called forth an unbearable longing to experience what he'd described.

He was staring down at her again, and she didn't know what to say. But it seemed words weren't needed. "I didn't think so."

Her throat was dry, but she didn't understand the reason. "What..." She had to lick her lips again before she could continue. She didn't miss the way his gaze settled on that small movement. "What is your wager?"

"You said you're not interested in marrying again."

"One kiss and an impressive amount of confidence is unlikely to change that."

His smile widened. "What if I can change your mind?"

Why did every man believe they were the answer to every woman's deepest desire?

Pushing down the traitorous inner voice that told her this one just might be correct, she pressed her lips together and arched against where his erection was still pressing into her. His small hiss told her she'd surprised him.

"I can tell that you're willing to try."

"You're a tempting little minx, do you know that?"

A thrill of pleasure streaked through her. He found her tempting? She had to know if he was playing with her, the same way Mansfield had tried to toy with her emotions before moving on to yet another paramour.

"I'm sure you say the same to all women. Is that enough to get them to let you have your way with them?"

"I won't pretend to be an innocent, but neither are you. I can assure you that no other woman has ever vexed me half as much."

"Because I'm not willing to fall into your bed with the crook of a finger?"

"Because your brother is going to kill me."

She couldn't hold back her laughter. It was true that Alex was being particularly overbearing when it came to the men who were sniffing around her. She'd seen him glaring at most of her dance partners last night, something for which she supposed she should be grateful. It meant no one had tried to drag her into another room during the ball to try his luck at forcing a seduction.

"What is your wager, my lord?"

He pulled back then, just enough to allow a few scant inches between their bodies. But her hands still rested on his shoulders, and his hands cupped her elbows.

"If I can bring you to release, you'll allow me to court you."

Her mind stuck on the second part of his statement. Shaking her head, she pulled away. To her relief, he let go of her immediately.

"I already told you I don't wish to marry again."

His hands hung loosely at his sides, but she could see the lines of tension in the way he held himself. A part of her expected him to yell at her now. It's what her husband would have done when he didn't get his way.

"I'm merely asking for the opportunity to court you. The decision about whether to accept me will lie solely with you."

Her heart was racing, but not because she was afraid of Holbrook. Her husband would have been yelling at her by now if she'd dared to defy him in such a manner. He would be hurling insults at her and belittling her.

The fact that Holbrook was giving her the power in this arrangement gave her pause.

She was no longer a young woman who'd be forced to marry because she'd been compromised. Widows—nay, even married women—took lovers with an alarmingly casual indifference, and no one seemed to care.

She could try this. She could allow this handsome, intriguing man to court her. But she was only now realizing that she hadn't heard the first part of his wager.

She straightened to her full height and clasped her hands at her waist as she faced him. "I'm afraid

I heard nothing beyond your desire to court me. What was your wager?"

He held his arms behind his back, and she had the unsettling realization that he was holding himself in check so he wouldn't reach for her again. Despite the tension that was still visible in his body, she could see that he was amused by her.

"You will allow me to court you if I can bring you to release."

Her brows furrowed in confusion. "You will release me?"

CHAPTER 8

ow on earth was it possible this woman didn't know what that word meant when it came to relations between a man and a woman? Her husband was the worst sort of bounder if he'd never seen to his wife's pleasure. Perhaps that was why he'd had so many lovers. No one wanted to sleep with him more than once.

"I will, of course, release you if you decide you don't want to have anything to do with me."

He ignored the internal voice that was shouting about how he was lying to her. He would never force her, but that didn't mean he wasn't above seducing her. Especially since she'd been the one to propose a love affair.

There was also the uncomfortable realization that Lucy Mansfield could very well be the one for him. Still, he didn't want to scare her away. He would have to proceed with caution.

He continued his explanation. "But the term *release* has another meaning when it comes to intimate relations between two people."

He wondered if he would have to spell it out for her, but the flush of color that rose in her cheeks told him she'd figured it out.

"But a woman can't… *release* with a man."

The sudden image of plunging into Lucy and giving her his seed threatened his composure. As it was, he was barely hanging on to his need to drag her into his arms again. She'd enjoyed their kiss, and he suspected she wouldn't mind a repeat performance, but he was playing a long game and couldn't rush things. If he wasn't careful, he'd lose this opportunity to make her his altogether.

"Pleasure, my temptress. The sudden release of sensation within your body when you've reached the heights of ecstasy."

Her eyes widened. Then she licked her lower lip again, and he wanted to groan with frustration. The fall of his trousers had been uncomfortably tight since he'd kissed her.

He saw the way her throat worked as she swallowed, and an irrational fear gripped him. She was going to change her mind and walk away.

"I… don't think that's possible. I've never found pleasure in the act of… I don't think I'm able to." She let out an embarrassed huff.

"I don't believe that's true. You might not have found release with your husband, but that doesn't mean you can't. Just that your husband was a selfish bastard who thought only of his own pleasure."

She stilled, her gaze lowered to the floor, and he wanted to kick himself. He'd never met Mansfield, but despite the fact he hated what he'd heard about the man, it was possible she still loved him.

"I apologize. I… don't really know what to say, but I shouldn't have spoken ill of the dead."

She wrapped her arms around her waist, and he expected her to turn away. Instead, she lifted her gaze to his. "I hated him. Not at first. When we married, I foolishly thought I was the most fortunate woman in the world. But it didn't take long for him to play me for a fool."

She turned toward the windows, and he wanted to put his fist through a wall. "He was the fool, not you. Any man who had you but failed to treasure you…"

He took a deep breath and unclenched his fists. Their conversation had taken an unpleasant turn. The last thing he needed was for Lucy to be thinking about another man even if he was her deceased husband. No, he wanted her to think only of him.

He moved so he was standing before her again, taking heart from the fact she was still here, talking to him.

"Lucy…"

She shook her head and dropped her arms. His heart plunged.

"Your wager is one-sided," she said. "What do I get if I win?"

He smirked, relief flooding through him. "Why would you want to win and deny yourself the pleasure I can give you?"

She laughed. "How are all men so confident?"

By way of reply, he held out a hand. The offer had been made, and now she would accept. But silence stretched to what felt like an eternity, and he could see the war she now waged within herself. She wanted to accept his wager, but uncertainty had her hesitating.

"Pleasure, Lucy. But just for you."

Her mouth formed a small *o* of surprise.

"What? How is that...?" She shook her head. "Never mind—it's clear I have much to learn."

To his relief, she placed her hand in his.

"We shall start with kisses."

She tilted her head to one side as though giving his words grave consideration. "I suppose I can suffer through that."

Her smile was teasing as she came into his arms and lifted her face to him, and triumph surged within him. The widowed Baroness Mansfield didn't know it yet, but she would soon be his.

He wanted to start with slow, teasing kisses as he'd done before, but Lucy was having none of that. She took the lead, and he was happy to allow it since it meant she would take what she wanted from him.

The soft mewl of pleasure she made as their tongues warred within his mouth had his already painful erection hardening further.

She gripped the back of his head, her fingers curling against his scalp and holding him in place. When she pressed herself more firmly against him, he groaned. Slowly, he traced a path of kisses along her jaw until he finally reached the small shell of her ear.

"May I touch you, Lucy?"

She shivered as he nuzzled the soft skin where her jaw ended. "You're touching me now."

He was indeed, but it wasn't nearly enough. He needed more, especially if he was going to give her the release he'd promised.

Taking her words as assent, he lowered one of his hands to cup her backside and pressed her more firmly into his erection. It took an extraordinary amount of willpower not to rock into her softness, but he'd promised her this was going to be about her. If he started rutting against her now, he risked scaring her away.

Her breath hitched but she didn't protest, and so he cupped a breast with his other hand.

She stiffened immediately, so he kept his touch light.

"I'm afraid," she said.

He wanted to curse but instead lifted his head to meet her gaze. "The moment you ask me to stop, I will."

She stared at him intently, as though trying to decide if she believed him.

"Do you trust me?" That was the crux of the matter after all. If she didn't trust him, if she couldn't relax with him, he wouldn't force the matter. He'd just have to take more time to coax her.

"I probably shouldn't, but… I do."

He closed his eyes briefly, relief sweeping through him. He couldn't deny that he was awed by her bravery. She clearly thought she was being a fool, but he vowed to prove himself worthy of her trust.

"I need to touch you to bring you pleasure. Intimately. Do you wish me to continue?"

She pressed her face into his shoulder, and he waited. Finally, after what seemed an eternity, she nodded. "Yes." Her voice was muffled against the fabric of his tailcoat.

Breathing out a sigh of relief, he stroked the breast he still held, his thumb lightly brushing against the underside. He half expected her to stiffen against him again, but instead, she let out a soft sigh and pressed her mouth against his jaw above the edge of his cravat.

Desire rocked through him when her tongue darted out to sweep against the skin there. By way of reply, he brushed his thumb against her nipple, circling it with the lightest of touches.

Her breath hitched, and that was all the encouragement he needed to continue.

He kept his touch light, soft caresses of both her breasts now. She might not have found release in her husband's bed, but it was clear her body yearned for it.

She was rocking against his cock now, and he returned the motion. Her soft, breathy murmur of assent had him continuing his assault. One hand remained at her breast while the other trailed ever so slowly down to her waist, then her hip. He was kissing her again, rewarded by her fervent response, when he began to inch up the fabric of her dress.

He drew back and allowed a fraction of space between their mouths. "I'm going to touch you between your legs, but only with my hand. Do you still want me to continue?"

She drew back, and her brow was furrowed again as she weighed the request. "Only your hands?"

"Yes."

"Can you kiss me while you do it?" Her voice was barely above a whisper.

"I'd kiss you forever if you'd allow me the privilege."

Her laugh was short, shaky, and it was clear she'd surprised herself that she could find anything about this situation amusing.

"You haven't won your wager yet, my lord."

His breath mingled with hers as he spoke against her plush lips. "No, but I will."

There was no soft exploration now. He couldn't take her body, but he could have her kisses, and so he plundered her mouth, his desire reaching a fever pitch as they drowned in each other. She was grasping his shoulders now, and he braced her against him with one hand low on her back as he trailed a path up her inner thigh.

When he reached her folds, she was wet for him.

Her breath stuttered as he stroked her there, just above her opening, where she was most sensitive. He continued his assault on her senses, and when her breath hitched again, he plunged one finger inside her. His thumb continued stroking that small bundle of nerves.

It didn't take long before she wrenched her mouth from his, her lips falling open with a soft cry as her entire body stiffened. He could feel the pulses of her release against the finger that was still inside her, and he wanted to shout out a cry of victory.

All too soon it was over. He allowed the fabric of her dress to fall again, and he took her mouth in another long, lingering kiss before allowing her to rest her head against his shoulder. He held her like that for some time.

"I didn't know." Her voice was soft against his body; then she tilted her head back. "I didn't know that was possible. And you didn't even..." She reached down to cover his erection with one hand, and he almost spilled in his trousers.

He grasped her wrist to stop her from bringing him to an embarrassing finish and brought her hand to his mouth. "Today was all about you."

Lucy's entire world had just turned upside down.

Now she understood why her married friends were so happy. Clearly their husbands shared the same intimate knowledge that Holbrook possessed.

Which left her wondering if Mansfield hadn't known how to please a woman or if he just hadn't cared about seeing to her needs. Given his general selfishness, she suspected it was the latter.

Holbrook took his leave after dropping a soft kiss on her lips and promising to call again. She watched him go without a word and then made her way to the armchair he'd recently occupied. A befuddled haze had settled over her senses, and she wasn't sure what she wanted to do about it.

Now she knew exactly what lay behind the many different ways her brother and her friends showed their love for their spouses. The casual touch of hands, a warm smile that seemed to convey things Lucy hadn't understood. The way they stood a little too close to one another, their lingering gazes and whispered conversations.

It seemed every one of them possessed the knowledge that marital relations didn't have to be one-sided. That women could have just as much pleasure from the marriage bed as their husbands.

Lucy drank the rest of her tea and then poured another cup. At least her hands weren't shaking. But given the lassitude that had settled over her body after Holbrook had brought her to release, she was surprised she didn't drop the teacup.

When she finished the second cup, she placed it carefully on the table before settling back into the armchair with a contented sigh. She knew she'd play every moment of her encounter with Holbrook over and over in her mind tonight. But first she needed to do something she found even more diffi-cult than approaching a man she barely knew and proposing an affair.

She needed to break the cardinal rule that had been in place since the moment her closest friend had fallen in love with her brother. She had to question Charlotte about her love life because it was now very clear to Lucy that her knowledge in that area was woefully inadequate.

CHAPTER 9

$\mathcal{H}$olbrook wanted to court her.

To *court* her.

It was the opposite of what Lucy had wanted when she decided to approach him about having an affair. Although, given the way he'd watched her during the Clarington ball, she might have found herself facing this same dilemma even if she hadn't reached out to him first.

The courtship would be an inconvenience, but she didn't regret what had transpired between them. The opposite was true—she'd been unable to think of little else.

She should have insisted there could be no possibility of him courting her. What had possessed her to accept his wager?

You'd been considering that perhaps Holbrook would show you what you've been missing all these years.

Lucy stared at her reflection in the dressing table mirror after dismissing her maid. The young woman had helped her into a flattering medium-blue dress trimmed with white flowers for that afternoon's excursion. After spending the past year in black, it was still strange to see herself in lighter colors. The woman staring back at her looked younger. Happier.

With a sigh, she opened the top drawer of the dressing table and took out the note Holbrook had sent her that morning.

I hope you will grant me the pleasure of taking you for a drive this afternoon.
—Holbrook

The devil had actually underlined the word *pleasure*, which told her he was also thinking about what they'd done yesterday.

She shouldn't have been surprised by his impudence, but she couldn't hold back her blush when Charlotte read the note over her shoulder. The

shrewd look in her friend's eyes told her that Charlotte knew exactly to what he was referring.

Fortunately her friend hadn't commented on
Holbrook's phrasing. Given the eye-opening conversation they'd had yesterday, Lucy was still reeling
from the fact she'd been married for eleven years
and somehow knew very little about the act of lovemaking. But given the small taste of delight she'd
experienced at Holbrook's hands, she couldn't wait
to experience more.

Holbrook called promptly at the appointed time.
She took his arm as they left the house, and he led her
to his open carriage. She couldn't resist the temptation
to lean a little too close to him, enjoying the feel of his
strong arm and remembering how he'd touched her.

It was ridiculous how excited she was for the
opportunity to spend time with him again. The
temperature was mild for April and there were birds
singing, but the man standing next to her, handing
her into his carriage, eclipsed everything else. They
both wore gloves, so there was nothing scandalous
in taking his hand as he helped her into the
carriage. Yet memories of how he had touched her
yesterday assailed her at the simple gesture.

When he climbed onto the seat next to her and

took up the reins with a smile, she was powerless to keep from returning it. If she didn't gain control of herself, everyone would soon be witnessing her all but swooning over this man.

She faced forward as she tried to tamp down her too-wide grin. They were in an open carriage, and in only a few minutes they'd be arriving at Hyde Park during the fashionable hour. It would be crowded, and if she couldn't control the breathless excitement threatening to overtake her just from sitting so close to Holbrook, it would be akin to making a public announcement about their relationship. People would talk.

Did she even care? It wasn't as though anyone would censure her. But it seemed a little unfair that they might become the subject of intense speculation before they'd shared a bed.

Although remembering her conversation with Charlotte yesterday, she supposed a bed wasn't strictly necessary.

Holbrook glanced at her before looking back at the horses. "I was disappointed you weren't at the Henderson ball last night. I'm thankful the duke and duchess were there because they saved me the trouble of searching everywhere for you."

She let out a surprised chuckle as she pictured

him running from one event to another. Surely he wouldn't actually have left the ball to go in search of her. On any given evening there were a number of events, both public and private. And that wasn't even counting the theater or the opera.

She gave him what she hoped was an arch look. "Why didn't I know you were such a flatterer?"

He glanced sideways at her. His grin was still in place, but now it was subdued. "I'm speaking the truth. Tell me, Lucy, were you hiding from me last night? Have you changed your mind about us?"

She hadn't given him permission to use her given name, but after the intimacies they'd shared yesterday, she wasn't going to chastise him for taking that liberty. Besides, she liked the way her name sounded in his deep tone. It reminded her of the moment he'd asked her if he could touch her.

A shiver of delight raced through her. Still, she wasn't so carried away with her memories that she couldn't see he was worried. Given their very different reasons for conducting this relationship, she could understand why he'd ask.

"You won the wager, my lord. I am honor bound to uphold my end of it."

He was concentrating now on bringing the carriage safely into the park. And luck was on their side because it seemed they were one of the first to arrive. Which meant the two lines forming between his brows was due to her failed attempt to keep their conversation lighthearted. She hated that she'd caused him even a moment of concern.

She placed a hand on his forearm, and he glanced at her. "I have no reservations about our present course of action even though we don't agree on the future outcome."

Her heart lightened when his expression cleared.

"It's early days yet. We'll worry about the future later. For now, I plan to enjoy our time together."

So did she. But she couldn't resist the temptation to tease him. "My brother knows about us."

When he winced, she had to bite her cheek to keep from laughing aloud.

"Don't tell me one of the servants heard us and rushed to tell him what happened. Should I expect to be called out?"

She thought he was teasing, but then she saw his frown. "Are you worried?"

"Of course. I've seen your brother when he's angry."

Alex wouldn't physically harm Holbrook. If he had allowed Mansfield to continue with his affairs

—albeit begrudgingly—he certainly wouldn't call Holbrook out for bringing her happiness. But it was undeniable Alex had the power to make the viscount's life very uncomfortable.

"You can relax. When he learned you'd called yesterday, Charlotte told him you're courting me. We'll allow him to continue thinking that."

"I *am* courting you."

Her smile was sheepish. "I suppose you are."

"I'll speak to him. Let him know my intentions are honorable."

"And then I'll let him know that any decision about whether I'll marry again rests solely with me."

Holbrook leaned close until their shoulders touched. "I'll do my best to make myself indispensable to you. I'll devote my every waking hour to ensuring you are satisfied—"

She covered her face with her hands, unable to look at him. The images conjured by his low, seductive voice—images of things she now knew they could do together—was almost too much to bear.

She peeked between her fingers when he laughed at her dismay, then dropped her hands and glared at him. "You are incorrigible."

"Would you want me any other way?"

No, she wouldn't. God help her, but she might want this man just a little too much.

The carriage had slowed to a crawl, and she realized that while they'd been talking, the park had begun to fill with other vehicles. She glanced around, wondering if any of their friends were here. It was a shock to realize that most of the men present were all but staring at them.

She glanced at Holbrook and lowered her voice. "We seem to be attracting a lot of attention."

One corner of his mouth kicked up in his lopsided smile. "That's hardly surprising given I'm here with the most desirable woman. They're probably plotting my demise so they can get to you."

He was so ridiculous that she couldn't hold back her laughter. "Don't worry—I'll protect you."

CHAPTER 10

Holbrook's carriage came to a halt in front of the Clarington town house. But instead of climbing down, he stared at the carriage door, examining the odd sense of restlessness that had settled over him. It took him several seconds to realize that the churning feeling in his stomach meant he was actually nervous.

He couldn't remember the last time he'd been this apprehensive. Probably when he'd arrived at Eton at the age of thirteen and come face-to-face with the reality that for the foreseeable future, he'd be spending more time at the school than at home with his family.

It was damn annoying.

With a deep breath, he did his best to ignore the inconvenient emotion and exited the carriage.

When he'd had dinner here a few days earlier, he'd been one of many people. Tonight he was the sole guest, and Clarington would be judging his worthiness to court his sister. Holbrook knew his intentions were honorable, but because of the misery Lucy's first husband had caused her, he'd need to prove himself to her brother.

He liked Clarington, who was a decade older than him. But he'd be lying if he said the man didn't intimidate him.

He lifted the heavy brass ring of the door knocker and let it fall against the brass plate. Clearly the action hadn't been necessary—the butler admitted him immediately and was probably already aware Holbrook's carriage had arrived.

The older man informed him that the family was waiting for him in the drawing room. He ignored the irrational urge to pull out his pocket watch to check whether he'd kept them all waiting.

He thanked the man and crossed the few steps to the drawing room, maintaining a measured pace as he took in another deep, steadying breath.

This was just another dinner party after all. He couldn't recall how many he'd been to over the years. *But never before with the family of the woman he wished to marry. They'd be judging everything he said and did.*

It appeared he wasn't going to be able to will away his nerves. He'd heard a well-known actor once say that he handled his stage nerves by telling himself they weren't a sign of fear. That they were, in fact, a sign he was excited about taking that first step out onto the stage. Once that step was taken, he was committed to the play and soon became the character, and all his fears were forgotten.

Holbrook could do this. He wasn't afraid of Clarington. He was merely excited to be taking this first important step toward his future with the woman he wanted to marry. The swooping sensation in his gut was just an invisible manifestation of his anticipation.

He took that last step and crossed the threshold into the drawing room.

The duke and duchess were sitting next to one another on the settee, their heads tilted toward each other. The duchess must have just said something amusing because Clarington laughed. It was obvious to everyone who saw the pair together that they were still very much in love despite the fact they'd been married for thirteen years.

Lucy was seated in an armchair and was also smiling at what the duchess had said. Holbrook tried not to wonder if she'd been sharing ideas about how to torture him tonight.

As one, their heads swiveled in his direction and Holbrook bowed.

"Your Graces, my lady. I was honored to receive your dinner invitation."

The women stood and dropped into polite curtsies. Clarington unfolded himself at a more leisurely pace, the weight of his full attention now on Holbrook.

"I'm pleased at your promptness," Clarington said. "I detest a late dinner guest."

Holbrook made some innocent remark by way of reply, but he couldn't say what it was. His attention had settled on Lucy, and there was something in the way she was looking at him that spoke louder than any words. She was desperate to speak to him.

But before she could say a word, Clarington clapped him on the shoulder. "Come."

Holbrook obeyed, of course. He wanted Clarington's good opinion if he was to gain his approval to court Lucy. Despite the fact the duke's sister was of age and free to spend time with whomever she wished, Clarington had the power to make things difficult.

He'd heard rumors of Clarington's displeasure at the way his brother-in-law treated his sister. Some even speculated about how he'd made a deal with the devil to bring about that final duel that had resulted in Mansfield's death, but Holbrook dismissed that as idle gossip. It had only been a matter of time, after all, before Lucy's husband slept with the wrong man's wife.

Neither spoke until they'd reached Clarington's study. Holbrook closed the door behind him since it was clear the man wanted privacy for this conversation.

"Have a seat," Clarington said as he settled into one of the two burgundy armchairs tucked into a corner of the room.

Holbrook sank into the chair. Perversely, this private conversation helped to settle his nerves. He'd much rather get straight to the reason he was here tonight instead of worrying all evening about what Clarington was thinking.

"I was glad to receive your invitation," Holbrook said, steepling his fingers at his waist. "It saved me the trouble of petitioning for an audience."

Clarington didn't reply right away. His arms were folded across his chest, his eyes narrowed as he examined Holbrook. He had the uncanny certainty that the duke was trying to see into his very soul.

Finally, after what seemed an eternity, Clarington spoke. "You know why you're here."

Holbrook nodded. "Because of my interest in your sister."

"I've been told you're courting her."

Holbrook settled his hands on the arms of the chair. "I assure you that my intentions are honorable."

To his surprise, Clarington winced. "That's going to be difficult. I'm sure you're aware that my sister has no intention of marrying again."

"She told me so herself."

"Is she aware you're courting her?"

Holbrook let out a wry chuckle. "Yes."

Clarington raised one brow. "And you've received her consent to do so?"

He smiled, remembering every detail of the wager he'd made with Lucy. "It wasn't easy, but yes, I've received her consent to court her. Not that she thinks there's any point to the endeavor."

Clarington shook his head and let out a low

humph. "I don't know how you managed that. And quite frankly, I don't think I want to know."

Holbrook was thankful for that. The last thing he needed was to be called out by Lucy's brother.

"I've been told you're a good man," Clarington continued. "There are many among my acquaintance who are quite fond of you."

Holbrook shrugged. "I find it easier to court friendships than to behave in a manner that would make many my enemy."

Unlike Mansfield. The words hovered, unspoken, in the air between him and the duke.

Clarington leaned back in his chair. "Their wives are also fond of you."

A frisson of alarm streaked through him. "I assure you that my actions have been honorable. I would never—"

Clarington let out a bark of laughter. "No, no, I didn't mean to insinuate otherwise. Besides, they're all happily married and it's clear they want to see you similarly settled."

"To be completely honest, when I was here before your ball, I had no intention of seeking a wife this season. It did occur to me that perhaps that time was drawing near, but it wasn't a priority."

There was a knowing smile on the duke's face. "What changed?"

"I had the pleasure of sitting next to your sister during that dinner and getting to know her better. And somehow by the end of the ball the next day, I realized that I wanted to get to know her *much* better."

He wondered if Clarington was aware that his sister was seeking a lover. But he wasn't foolish enough to voice the question.

Clarington's smile was now a grin. "And you've decided that you want to marry my sister."

Holbrook nodded. "I'm not ready to offer for her. She's not there yet, but I plan to sway her to my way of thinking. We need to get to know one another better first."

"You're going to find it difficult to convince Lucy to give marriage another try. Mansfield was a bastard."

Holbrook wholeheartedly agreed. He'd heard enough rumors to have a vivid impression of just what type of man Lucy's husband had been.

"I will do everything in my power to change her mind."

Clarington's eyes narrowed again. "I'll be watching you."

Holbrook nodded. "Your sister has already suffered through one unhappy marriage. I would think less of you if I believed you were willing to allow her to enter into a second one. Especially since it's clear you, yourself, are very happily married."

Clarington nodded and stood. He held out his arm. Holbrook rose to his feet and shook his hand.

"We are in agreement then. I will kill you if you hurt my sister."

Holbrook nodded. "I wouldn't have it any other way."

"Good. We should make our way back before Lucy barges in here. She's informed me that I have exactly five minutes to speak with you. Any longer and she'll assume I'm torturing you."

CHAPTER 11

*L*ucy needed to know what was happening in her brother's study. If not for Charlotte, she'd be outside the room right now, her ear pressed to the heavy wooden door. But her best friend was adamant about Lucy leaving the two men to their discussion.

She rose to her feet and began to pace. Charlotte watched her—no doubt to ensure she didn't storm into the study—but said nothing. She couldn't explain why she was so worried.

She glanced at the clock over the fireplace mantel. They'd left the room two minutes ago, and she was beset with worry about what was happening. Alex was being insufferably overprotective of her. She could understand why, but that didn't mean she had to like it.

Perhaps she should have told her brother that she was the one who'd propositioned Holbrook. And that he'd turned down her suggestion they have an affair, insisting instead that he wanted to court her.

No, she couldn't do that. She wouldn't be the reason Holbrook was ostracized from his circle of friends.

But maybe her brother wouldn't care as long as Holbrook made her happy.

"You're making me dizzy," Charlotte said, intruding on her spiraling thoughts.

"I'm a widow, for heaven's sake. Holbrook shouldn't need to ask for permission to court me."

Charlotte was clearly trying not to laugh at her very real concern. "I doubt very much that Holbrook is asking for permission. But I can't guarantee that Alex won't threaten to call him out if he hurts you."

Lucy threw herself onto the settee next to her friend.

Charlotte wrapped an arm around her shoulders in a sideways hug. "Why are you so worried? I haven't heard anything that would lead me to believe there's any danger of Holbrook acting dishonorably. I've made several discreet inquiries on the matter."

Lucy shouldn't have been so surprised, yet she was. "When? Why?"

"Before we invited him to dinner on the eve of the ball, of course. As the only single gentleman on the guest list, I wanted to ensure I wasn't inviting a snake into our midst."

"Like Mansfield."

Charlotte looked away. "Exactly." She forced a smile and faced Lucy again. "But everyone said complimentary things about him. And if Ladies Cranston and Hargrove are to be believed, he played an instrumental role in helping their husbands overcome their reluctance to marriage."

Lucy hadn't heard anything about that. "So he's a matchmaker?"

Charlotte laughed. "Not as far as I know. But apparently he does have a steady nature and is very good at seeing what one is trying to hide under the surface."

Lucy felt a spark of alarm. Had Holbrook been able to see what she'd been trying to hide? That she was unhappy and felt a tiny bit jealous of her friends' marriages?

She let out a soft sigh. Of course he had. She suspected everyone knew that.

The clock struck eight, and Lucy shook off her reverie. It had been more than five minutes. She should go see whether Holbrook was still here or if he'd escaped out a side entrance. The thought that he would give up on her had her jumping to her feet.

"I should go check on them…"

Charlotte grasped her arm, preventing her escape. "They're coming."

Lucy listened and realized her friend was right. The soft murmur of deep voices, growing louder by the second, reassured her that Holbrook hadn't fled.

"You should have seen the look on his face when I told him I wasn't going to support his bill," Alex said.

Holbrook was clearly amused when he replied. "No doubt it was the same sour expression he donned for the rest of that session."

Both men were laughing when they entered the drawing room. Holbrook's gaze sought her out immediately. He winked.

And Lucy's heart turned over in her chest.

CHAPTER 12

Lucy was driving him to distraction. Two weeks had passed since their first ride in Hyde Park, and Holbrook's certainty about her had only grown. His heart was fixed on having her forever.

When he'd witnessed Cranston and Hargrove wrestle with their feelings about the women who would become their wives, he'd done what he could to help them overcome their reluctance. But it was an unsettling sensation to find himself on the other side of that equation. Especially when he found himself doubting he'd be able to convince her to marry him.

He'd never enjoyed a woman's company quite so much, and the more time he spent with the widowed baroness, the more intrigued he became. He wanted to know everything about her—her likes and dislikes and her opinions on all manner of things.

It was more than a little surprising just how often he thought about her.

She was unlike any woman he'd ever known. He hadn't lied when he'd told her that he'd had love affairs but there hadn't been anyone he'd ever wanted to see more than a handful of times. As far as he knew that casual indifference had been reciprocated by every one of those women. But despite her insistence that she only wanted a love affair, Lucy always seemed genuinely happy to see him.

They'd made a point of attending the same entertainments over the past weeks. When she told him which invitations she'd accepted, she teased him by saying she didn't want him racing through London searching for her. He hadn't denied the accusation because he would have done just that.

There'd been balls, routs, musicales. Once, during a play—he couldn't remember the name because he'd been so distracted by Lucy, who'd been one of the theatergoers sharing his box—she'd tugged him to one side during the intermission. He'd leaned close to hear what she was saying above the conversations taking place around them, and she told him that the theater box next to theirs was empty.

He'd raised his brows, thinking that surely she wasn't suggesting what he was imagining. But her wicked smile in response told him why she'd chosen to share that piece of information with him.

When they returned to their seats, she gave his arm a little tug as they were passing the empty box. And everything inside him screamed at him to accept her invitation.

The all-too-brief taste of pleasure he'd given her that first afternoon when he'd called on her had only whetted his appetite. He wanted to do so much more with her. To give in and engage in the love affair she'd told him she wanted.

But Holbrook was playing a long game. He couldn't deny he worried that if they made love, she'd take what enjoyment he could give her before moving on to another man. It was an irrational fear since she'd given no indication she was interested in someone else's attention.

And he was very aware of just how many *were* interested.

Which was why he found himself standing on the edge of a ballroom that evening and watching her dance with another man. Not just any dance—a waltz.

Since they weren't wed, he wasn't able to remain at Lucy's side. Because of that, he found himself standing on the opposite end of the ballroom when he heard the opening strains of the waltz. He sought her out, of course, but it was too late. She'd already accepted another's invitation, and the man was leading her onto the dance floor.

He tamped down his frustration and resisted the urge to barge between them and drag Lucy away. He was courting her, yes, but they hadn't made any promises aside from agreeing not to have physical relations with anyone else. And waltzing could hardly be seen as a betrayal of that promise.

He didn't recognize her partner, which meant he was probably a second or third son. Even if they weren't personally acquainted, he knew most of the titled gentlemen on sight from those endless sessions in Parliament. There were a few who didn't take their responsibilities seriously, ignoring their duties to the House of Lords, but he knew those gentlemen as well.

He supposed the younger man could have been a baronet, but his position in the ton didn't really matter. He was dancing with Lucy, bringing her body a little too close to his and all but leering at her.

It would be unbearably rude to interrupt and drag her away from the impudent youth, but Holbrook might be able to carry it off. He inched closer to where they were moving together. The ball was crowded, and it was possible he'd be able to come between them and whisk her away before anyone realized what he was doing.

And even if anyone witnessed his churlish behavior, it certainly wouldn't be the worst thing to happen in the midst of a crowded ball. No worse than the handful of men who were even now pressing themselves crudely into their partners.

He saw the stumble that proceeded Lucy's wince and he had no doubt the youth—was he even of age? He seemed ridiculously young to be there—had caused it. Having danced several times with her, he'd never seen her falter in such a manner.

He was considering pushing his way through the middle of the dance floor when he saw her take a step back and curtsy.

They were leaving the dance floor early. Relieved, he continued his circuitous route around the room. He was so close, but waltzing couples kept passing between him and his target and he lost sight of them.

When he reached the side of the room where Lucy and her partner had been headed, he didn't see her. The young man was also missing.

His eyes darted to the open garden doors that were only a few feet away. He couldn't help but remember the Clarington ball when he'd worried needlessly that someone had spirited her away into the gardens. He'd been mistaken that time, but Lucy wasn't in her own home now. His instincts were telling him to head outside.

He quickened his pace and exited onto the terrace, his eyes roaming across the outdoor space in search of her.

He found Lucy at the bottom of the terrace steps. Her back was to him, but he recognized the gown she'd been wearing. It was yet another blue gown, this one so light it was almost white. He'd come to realize that blue was her favorite color.

She was standing at a strange angle, leaning forward a fraction. Not wanting to draw the attention of those standing just inside the garden doors, he crossed the space that separated them without a word.

A masculine curse had him breaking into a run and dashing down those stairs. But when he reached the bottom, he froze in place, shock taking hold as he took in the astonishing scene before him.

The young man was lying on the ground, face down. Lucy held the arm closest to her at an awkward angle behind his back. One slippered foot rested between his shoulder blades, and every time he struggled to get up, she twisted his arm further.

He must have made a sound because Lucy's head whipped around. When she saw him standing there, she gave him a strained smile.

"I was wondering what I should do next. Are you here to offer assistance, my lord?"

Another jerk of the young man's arm had him uttering a string of epithets. She dropped his arm and stepped back quickly, out of his reach.

"You belong in Bedlam," the man hissed as he struggled to his feet. He cradled the elbow of his abused arm in his other hand.

Lucy remained in place, her arms folded across her breasts and a fierce scowl on her face. "I may be a widow, but that doesn't mean you can take liberties with me. A gentleman asks first, and he takes no for an answer."

The man's immaculately coiffed hair had flopped down over his forehead. Holbrook didn't see any reason to mention the dirt that covered the front of his waistcoat. And his cravat was soiled beyond repair.

The youth made to brush past them, but Holbrook clamped a hand on his injured shoulder. Satisfaction surged through him at the youth's grunt of pain. "Leave now and I won't call you out tomorrow morning. And if you possess even an ounce of self-preservation, pray that I never see you near Lady Mansfield again."

He released his grip, and the youth scurried off. He was smart enough not to return to the ball, choosing to circle around the side of the house so he could make his exit.

Holbrook turned to stare at Lucy. He would have thought he'd imagined the entire incident, but she was still glaring after her would-be assailant.

"What...? How...? I don't understand."

She shifted and met his gaze. "Excuse me?"

Somehow he managed to gather his wits enough to speak. "I rushed out here in case you were in danger, but you had the situation in hand. How did you even know what to do? He could have overpowered you…" He shook his head, refusing to dwell on what-ifs.

Lucy grinned. "I've been taking lessons."

"Lessons? From whom?" And what type of lessons would have taught her how to take a man down in that fashion? Not fencing and certainly not boxing.

She shrugged, the movement casual. "The Countess of Brantford and her sister-in-law, the Duchess of Castlefield. They're providing private lessons to women on how to defend themselves when faced with unwanted advances. It's not widely advertised. Women are passing along the information to others."

He supposed it made sense. Brantford had a formidable reputation. Before he'd married, everyone had called him the Unaffected Earl. That moniker had lost favor over the years when it became obvious that he was utterly devoted to—and affected by—his wife.

Some thought he was a spy, but others called such speculation nonsense since he spent most of the year in London. But whatever the truth, it was evident the man had seen to it that his sister and his wife could handle themselves when faced with danger.

And apparently the two women had gone on to teach others how to do the same.

"Who told you about their lessons?"

"Charlotte has been attending for a couple of years. I've only just started. I don't think Mr. Larson expected me to defend myself or he would have been able to stop me. Thankfully, men are notorious for underestimating women."

Holbrook dragged her into his arms, hugging her to him for almost a full minute. When he finally collected himself, he stepped back but still held on to her hands. "Well, I for one am very thankful to the duchess."

With reluctance, he dropped her hands and offered her his arm. "Shall we return to the ball, my lady?"

She smiled up at him, a gleam in her eyes. "Or perhaps we should head into the gardens for a few minutes. Since we're already here, it would be a shame not to enjoy them."

It was sorely tempting. The Lord must have put Lucy Mansfield in this world just to test his willpower.

He held out his arm for her, intending to return to the ballroom. Eyebrows would rise when the two of them entered together, but as a widow, Lucy was free to spend time alone with a gentleman. He no longer cared that people would talk. She wouldn't be ruined, and there was no danger of her being ostracized by society.

When she tucked her hand into his elbow, he saw the slight tremor she was trying to hide. His eyes narrowed as he looked down at her, but she wouldn't meet his gaze. She was taking deep breaths, and he realized she was shaken by what had just happened.

Of course she was. He cursed himself and changed direction, taking them deeper into the garden. He took a few turns, glancing about to ensure there were no other couples looking for a few moments of privacy in the gardens. The last thing he needed tonight was to interrupt a clandestine tryst.

Not when he wanted nothing more than to be engaging in one himself with this woman.

He spotted a bench in a secluded bower and headed in that direction. He glanced at Lucy when they reached it, and she was smiling at him again. His heart turned over.

"You've changed your mind," she said as she settled onto the bench.

He sat next to her and placed an arm around

her shoulders. She leaned against him without a word of protest.

"I realized you might need a few minutes to settle your nerves before returning to the ballroom."

She shuddered. "I've practiced that move so often but never thought I'd actually have to use it. I didn't think, I just acted."

She needed to process the encounter in her own time, and so he didn't say another word. But he wanted to chase the youth down and smash his hand into his face. Perhaps he should call him out after all.

He was brought back to the present by her gloved hand settling against his cheek. "You're angry."

He pressed a kiss into her palm. "Not with you."

"Of course not. But you needn't worry about Mr. Larson. I doubt he'll trouble me again."

He forced his tense muscles to relax. "I hate that you were put in the position of needing to defend yourself against him."

She took hold of his hand, twining their fingers together. "It is the way of the world."

He raised their joined hands and turned them so he could place a kiss on the soft skin of her wrist above her white glove.

Her breath hitched and he looked up, meeting her gaze. Unable to resist, he licked her skin.

"Holbrook..."

He was only human. The hitch in her voice as she said his name on a soft breath had him hardening instantly. He reached for her shoulders and turned her carefully until they were facing each other. His eyes roamed over her face.

When he saw no hint of uncertainty, he kissed her. It was supposed to be a quick touch of his mouth to hers, just one taste, but her soft moan was nearly his undoing.

She deepened the kiss immediately, and he returned it with equal fervor. His hand was already on her breast when her gasp of pleasure had him freezing in place.

Every part of his body, every bone, every sinew, urged him to continue. But they were at a ball, and at any moment someone might stumble upon them.

He didn't know where he found the strength, but he forced himself to release her soft breast and raised his head. They stayed like that for several seconds, staring at each other, their breaths coming fast.

Finally Lucy sighed and framed his face between her hands. "You need to put us both out of our misery. How much longer are you going to keep denying what we both want?"

Until you say you'll be mine forever. But he wasn't foolish enough to say the words aloud.

CHAPTER 13

It was Wednesday, which meant Parliament wasn't in session. And as he'd done every Wednesday for the past month, he would be calling on Lucy to take her to Hyde Park. The open-air carriage was by far the safest way to spend time with her without giving in to the temptation to find a quiet corner and allow themselves to get carried away.

But since it was still too early in the day, he needed a distraction.

He was on top of the world when he entered White's. His courtship of the beautiful—and surprisingly resourceful—baroness was going according to plan. And after the incident in the garden with the young man who'd tried to take liberties with her, it seemed she was no longer worried about showing a preference for his company.

She still accepted requests to dance with other men, but if someone asked to partner her for a waltz, she informed them she'd already promised that dance to another. Because all her waltzes were now his.

He glanced across the men gathered in the morning room, hoping at least one of his close acquaintances was there. He smiled when he saw Hargrove and his brother-in-law, Baron Cranston, seated next to the unlit fireplace on the far end of the room. Their heads were close together, and when he approached, he realized their voices were low murmurs. It was obvious they were taking care not to be overheard.

When he drew near, he cleared his throat to gain their attention. He was about to apologize and ask if they wanted him to return later but hesitated when he saw the way they glanced at each other before shifting to look at him. There was something in their expressions that told him they'd been talking about him.

Still, good manners had him asking, "I hope I'm not interrupting."

Hargrove indicated an empty armchair. "Please join us."

Holbrook examined the pair as he sat. Their serious expressions warned him something was amiss. "Why the long faces?"

Cranston blew out a breath. "We're debating an important matter that concerns you."

Holbrook raised a brow and waited for him to continue.

After a few seconds, Hargrove spoke. "It relates to the widowed baroness and, by extension, you."

Holbrook waved off the footman who was approaching, his senses on high alert. "Lady Mansfield?"

Hargrove leaned back in his chair and folded his arms across his chest. "You're the one who insisted we tell him immediately."

Cranston frowned. "I think you should break the news."

Holbrook was going to bash both their heads together if one of them didn't tell him what was going on.

When Hargrove didn't reply, Cranston leaned forward and rested his elbows on his knees. "We've just learned that a bet has been placed."

Cranston didn't have to say anything else.

Holbrook knew exactly what he was talking about. The infamous White's betting book. Idle gentlemen with far too much time on their hands placed wagers on all manner of things.

Anger had him clenching his fists. "Someone placed a wager about Lucy?"

Cranston nodded. "They're betting on who will be the first to claim her as their mistress."

A haze of red descended over Holbrook's vision.

Hargrove leaned forward. "If it's any consolation, you've taken a commanding lead."

Holbrook swore. "Give me the name of the person who dared to put her name in that damned book."

Cranston frowned. "There was no name attached."

Hargrove shook his head. "Of course not. Making a bet about Clarington's sister is social suicide."

"Especially one that would tempt every ne'er-do-well to proposition his sister." Cranston shook his head. "Whoever it was, he'd better hope Clarington never learns his identity."

"We have to remove that bet." He tried not to think about how many men would force themselves on Lucy just so they could gain bragging rights. "The jackals are already circling her."

"Of course they are," Cranston said. "Even without that bet, she's highly desirable. Young, beautiful, supposedly barren. Add to that the fact she's the sister of a powerful duke?"

Holbrook tensed, ready to leap to his feet.

Cranston stopped him with a hand on his shoulder. "Easy, man. If you take any rash action, it will only cause more gossip."

Holbrook wanted to ignore the baron and demand the betting book be brought to him immediately. Then he wanted to compare the handwriting of the man who'd placed that bet against every member of the club.

What he did instead was will himself to relax. A quick glance told him they were beginning to attract attention, and Lucy was already at the center of far too much speculation.

Hargrove's eyes had a knowing glint in them. "Remember that prodding you gave me concerning Eleanor?"

Of course he did. Hargrove had been so turned around that he'd almost thrown away his chance at love.

"Unlike you, I'm actually courting the woman I love."

Cranston let out a low whistle, which Holbrook ignored.

"Then what are you waiting for?" Hargrove asked.

What indeed. "I'm trying to behave with honor."

Cranston shook his head. "Fuck honor. This is war. If you don't go on the offensive, you just might find yourself on the losing side."

Since the baron had spent years serving in the army, Holbrook wasn't surprised by his choice of analogy. Cranston was correct, but that didn't mean Holbrook had to like it. Even without that damned bet, every man—both scrupulous and not—would want Lucy. And since she hadn't fallen pregnant while married to Mansfield, most wouldn't even consider marrying her.

What exactly was he waiting for? What if Lucy tired of his courtship and approached someone else about having an affair? He almost snorted at the thought. She wouldn't even need to ask. All she'd have to do was send another man an encouraging glance and they would leap at the chance to be with her.

A spear of white-hot jealousy threatened to steal his breath. No. Lucy was his.

He rose to his feet.

"What are you going to do?" Hargrove asked.

"I'm going to give the lady in question what she wants."

The gloves were off. It was time to end the dance in which they'd been engaging for the past month. He was going to give Lucy Mansfield the pleasure she wanted from him.

She'd insisted she didn't want to marry again, and like a stubborn fool he'd been hoping she'd change her mind. But his stubbornness—his insistence on doing the *honorable* thing—might cause her to turn to another man.

Hell would freeze over before he allowed that to happen.

He was going to show Lucy that the attraction they both felt went far beyond mere lust. That their souls were bound together. And if he could only achieve that by ensuring she was addicted to his touch, so be it.

He was grinning when he left White's and climbed into his carriage.

CHAPTER 14

$\mathcal{L}$ucy's days had fallen into a comfortable pattern since the start of the season, and that was just how she enjoyed things. Her late husband had hated that about her, but she'd never been spontaneous and didn't enjoy making plans at the last minute.

Even during the hustle and bustle of the season with its heavy burden of social demands, Lucy knew what to expect every day. She broke her fast each morning with her brother, Charlotte, and her nieces and nephews. Afterward, the children would go up to the schoolroom for their lessons and Alex would be busy with the numerous demands placed on someone of his standing.

She and Charlotte would occupy themselves

with various tasks. Weekly lessons with Lady Brant-ford and the Duchess of Castlefield were a must, especially after Lucy discovered firsthand just how important it was to fend off the unwanted advances of men who refused to take no for an answer.

Mr. Larson had, at least, taught her that valu-able lesson. He couldn't have been more than one and twenty, and Lucy had made the mistake of thinking he was just being kind when he suggested they head out to the terrace for some air. But it seemed that all men, no matter how young or old, believed widows were easy prey.

Lucy shook off that distressing thought and focused on more pleasant ones. Holbrook would be calling today for their weekly drive in Hyde Park. It was a custom she looked forward to, primarily because it provided them with a measure of privacy. Even when they were in the middle of the park, with at least half the members of the ton either strolling along the path or in their carriages, they could lower their voices and have a private conversation.

Lucy took advantage of these weekly outings to try to tempt Holbrook into providing her with another sampling of the pleasure only he seemed capable of giving her. At this point she didn't even care if they made love. One month had passed since he'd brought her to release, and she was beginning to think that perhaps she'd dreamed the whole thing.

At the very least, he needed to show her just why she should change her mind about marrying him. Give her another taste of what marrying him would be like.

The errant thought had just passed through her mind when he arrived for their outing and she realized he was winning. His courtship was tempting *her* to change her mind when she'd hoped he would be the one to reconsider the type of relationship they could have.

She waved to the butler before leaving to meet Holbrook outside the town house. It was still strange that she could be unmarried and yet allowed such freedom to come and go as she pleased.

Holbrook led her a small way up the street. "I apologize for being late. I had to do something very important before our outing today."

There was an edge to his tone that had her glancing sideways at him. But he looked much the same as he always did. Tall, handsome, immaculately dressed. He turned to wink at her, and a thrill shot through her.

Something was different about him but she couldn't say what.

He stopped in front of a black carriage, and she looked at him in confusion. This wasn't his open-air carriage, the one that was appropriate for riding through Hyde Park. This carriage would enclose them while a carriage driver conveyed them to their destination. It would keep them away from prying eyes.

He smiled and opened the vehicle's door. He bent to lower the step and then held out his hand to help her in.

Anticipation was a living, breathing thing inside her as she placed her hand in his and climbed into the carriage. Still, she tried to be practical. This didn't mean anything—it couldn't. Holbrook had insisted on behaving like a gentleman. Perhaps something had happened to his other carriage and he hadn't been able to procure another open carriage for their drive today.

Was this also his carriage or had he borrowed it? She ran her fingers along the red leather interior, marveling at the plush feel of the cushions. It wasn't nearly as luxurious as her brother's carriages, but it was definitely of higher quality than the one her husband had purchased shortly after their marriage. With the way he'd spent money, her dowry hadn't lasted long before they'd had to make do with more practical purchases.

"Is this your carriage? Did something happen to the other one?"

He settled into the seat opposite her, and when she met his eyes, there was something in them she hadn't seen since their first time alone together. Heat.

Surely she was imagining things. Seeing what she wanted to see.

He didn't reply, and the air grew heavy between them. Finally, when the carriage began to move, he shocked her by leaning forward and closing the space between them.

"Holbrook?"

Before she was aware of what he intended to do, his large hands settled on her waist and he lifted her. She let out a small squeak of surprise before he settled her onto his lap.

She didn't chastise him since she was exactly where she wanted to be. Instead, she leaned against his broad chest, enjoying the way he circled his arms around her to keep her in place.

Silly man, did he think she'd want to be anywhere else?

"What is the meaning of such shocking familiarity, my lord?"

His eyes were almost black as he stared down at her in the dim light of the carriage. Before he said a word, she already knew she'd won.

"I've decided to give in to temptation."

The low rasp of his voice against her ear as he nuzzled the side of her throat caused gooseflesh to rise on her arms and desire to spear low in her belly.

She had a moment of sanity, remembering that what they were doing might be visible through the carriage windows. Anyone in a passing conveyance had only to glance through their windows and they'd be able to see exactly what was happening.

It was ironic that just as she was finally getting what she wanted, she felt compelled to put a stop to their intimacy.

"The windows are still open. And we can't ride through Hyde Park with the curtains pulled close—"

He grinned down at her, and her heart dipped into her belly.

"We're not going to Hyde Park, my sweet temptress."

She tilted sideways as he reached to close the curtains of first one, then the second window. His arms held her securely in place, but she kept a tight grip on his shoulders just in case.

"We're not?" Had her voice ever been so breathy before that moment?

"No. I'm taking you to my town house."

She was filled with questions. Why had he changed his mind? She'd known pleasure at this man's hands, and that brief glimpse of everything she'd been missing all these years had only served to whet her appetite.

But Holbrook had remained steadfast in his determination that he would not make love to her unless she accepted his suit. She'd worried he would continue to keep her at arm's length as long as they weren't legally wed.

So why now?

One of Holbrook's gloved hands caressed her cheek. Their gazes locked, and she could see concern reflected there.

"If I'm presuming…"

She shook her head. "No, of course not. I was

simply wondering why you'd changed your mind about the two of us being together."

"I realized that my stubbornness might cause me to lose you altogether."

His words were spoken with earnestness, but she couldn't hold back her laugh. Holbrook was delusional if he thought she was even slightly interested in any of those men who seemed intent on pursuing her.

"I'll tell you a secret, my lord."

His thumb caressed her lower lip, and a shiver went through her. "I do like the sound of that."

One small corner of her mind tried to warn her that it was unwise to place her trust in a man again. She ignored that inner voice. "I have no intention of propositioning another man."

One corner of his mouth quirked up. "That might be true today—and I'm heartened to hear it —but one never knows what the future holds. And you should know that I haven't given up on trying to change your mind. I'm still courting you."

He kissed her then, and she sank into him, drowning in the feel of his strong arms pulling her close. The hard length of his arousal pressed against her hip, telling her without a doubt that he wanted this as much as she did.

Holbrook had shown her that he knew just how to touch her to stoke her desire. But right now she wanted to show him that she was willing to share that pleasure. Today wasn't going to be about her but about the two of them. Together.

She worked one hand down to cup his hard length, and his breath hitched out in obvious surprise. She wanted to take time to explore him, unwilling to wait a moment longer, but the carriage was already slowing.

He lifted his head and stared down at her for several long seconds.

Slowly her senses began to clear, and she realized she'd almost gotten completely carried away in a carriage.

"Do you think it will be fine for the two of us to enter your town house together? I'm sure rumors are already swirling around us, but…"

"But you want to be discreet. I want that as well, which is why I instructed the carriage driver to bring us around to the mews at the back of the house."

She let out a sigh. That was marginally better. The servants would still know, but they always knew what was happening. Some might consider them invisible, but Lucy had always been aware of their watchful presence.

The carriage pulled into the small stable at the back of the house, and Holbrook climbed down first. When he helped her from the vehicle, she tried to ignore the stablehands who glanced their way before quickly looking away again.

She wondered if he made it a habit to bring women to his town house, but her mind shied away from the thought. She didn't want to know. They'd already agreed that while the two of them were together, there would be no other liaisons. She wanted to trust him to keep his word. More than that, she needed to believe he'd be faithful. She saw evidence that men were capable of fidelity in the relationships of her friends and family.

And if he wanted to see other women, they would end their affair.

A pang of something she chose not to examine speared through her at that thought.

She followed Holbrook along a paved path to an entrance at the side of the house and was relieved their arrival wouldn't be witnessed by his neighbors.

He opened the door, and she found herself on a small landing. The inner door on the other side of the landing would open to the rest of the rooms on the main floor. The stairs going down would lead to the kitchens. She was curious to explore his house, but that would have to wait for another time.

He took her hand and led her up the second set of stairs, which would take them to the bedrooms.

When Holbrook stopped outside his bedchamber, a man materialized from the other end of the hall. He didn't look like a footman, so she assumed it was Holbrook's valet.

Holbrook murmured instructions that they were not to be disturbed and then opened the door and ushered her into his bedroom.

She stood there, just inside the threshold, and took in the space. It was clear at a glance that this was a man's bedroom. The furniture was made of rich mahogany, and the fabrics were a deep blue.

His bed took up about a third of the room, and she immediately imagined the two of them rolling around in it. Surely she wouldn't be lying on one side, stiff, while he... No, she already knew that Holbrook would be far more creative in the bedroom than her husband had been.

Her gaze darted to the small sitting area to the left of the entrance—one armchair and a side table upon which were piled several books. She couldn't help but smile as she imagined him relaxing there, reading before turning in for the night.

Curiosity had her walking over to the table to examine the books. Her gaze skimmed over the two larger tomes and settled on the two novels. *A Fallen Lady* and *A Lady Redeemed*.

She picked up the latter. She'd read the first last year during her period of mourning but hadn't been aware the sequel had been released. "I didn't know you read novels."

He shrugged. "It's a newly acquired addiction. It helps that I know the author of those two books."

Her mouth dropped open, and she clutched the book to her chest. "You know who wrote this?" The novels were anonymously written. No one knew who the author was.

His smirk was maddening. "I'll allow them to make that public knowledge when they're ready. But I will say that it appears you're well on your way to learning the truth for yourself."

Her mind spun at the implication of his words. What did he mean? Did she know the author? She'd met a lot of people over the past month, but most were merely acquaintances. Aside from…

She gasped. "Was he there? During the dinner

party before Alex and Charlotte's ball?" Those were the only people she considered friends.

Holbrook shrugged, but his eyes glinted. "I can neither confirm nor deny that."

His words said one thing, but the edge to his voice told her she'd guessed correctly. Unless he was lying about the whole thing. "Are you teasing me?"

His smile was genuine as he plucked the book from her hands. He turned to the dedication and handed the book back to her. "No. But I find it interesting that you assumed the author is male."

She looked down at the book.

To my loving husband, who has been a source of inspiration and support.

She closed the book with a soft sigh. "You are most vexing, Holbrook."

He laughed. "If it's any consolation, I have it on good authority that the author's identity will be revealed later this season. But I'm sure she'll tell you herself soon enough."

She crossed her arms and glared at him. "So there's no reason you can't tell me now."

He shrugged. "It isn't my secret to tell. Now put the book down and come here. We're not here for a book discussion."

She fingered the slim volume. "I haven't read the sequel."

He took the book from her hands and set it atop the pile of books. Then he wrapped his arms around her. "You can take it with you when you leave. After I'm finished with you."

The low timbre of his voice was filled with dark promise, and a shiver raced through her.

"But if you've changed your mind—if you want more time to think about this—please tell me now. I know I was being presumptuous in bringing you here without discussing it with you first."

She stared at him, his longing clearly visible in the taut lines of his face. Now that he'd given in to what was happening between them, he wanted this as much as she did. But she also knew that he was a man of his word. If she told him she no longer wanted to make love to him, he would take her home.

She trusted him. She couldn't say why. Heaven knew she'd never been able to dissuade her husband when he was intent on taking his marital rights. But Holbrook would stop if she asked him to.

"I want to be here. I've imagined this so often since you first showed me what it meant to experience desire."

He closed his eyes in relief, and it humbled her that he would put her own needs above what he so clearly wanted.

"Did you think I'd changed my mind?"

"No. But it's important that you know I would never force you to do anything. Also…" One brow lifted. "You are a difficult woman to pin down."

"You haven't pinned me yet, my lord." Images of him lying over her and thrusting into her body filled her imagination.

She'd never enjoyed the act with her husband, but he'd never given any consideration to her pleasure. Holbrook, on the other hand, had been nothing but patient with her. He'd shown her that her body was capable of enjoying intimacy with a man and had demanded nothing in return.

Well, nothing except marriage. The thought of finding herself in another unhappy marriage had always sent a wave of cold panic through her. That she'd even considered changing her mind earlier today was testament to just how much she wanted this man.

But now she didn't have to worry about taking that chance. He could show her the pleasure he'd promised, and she was almost desperate with longing.

She leaned into the strength of his broad chest. "What happens now?" Her gaze shifted to his very large bed. Mansfield had always joined her in her bedroom, usually when she was already in bed. This affair was completely different, and she didn't know how to proceed. Her pulse was beginning to race. "Should I lie down on the bed?"

His brows drew together. "Do you think I'm going to throw you on the bed, lift your skirts, and rut inside you like a beast?"

The picture he painted was so close to what used to happen with Mansfield that she should have been horrified. But thinking of Holbrook hovering over her, touching her first to ensure she was ready for him, seeing to her pleasure, sent a rush of wetness between her legs.

She couldn't help but remember the taunt her husband had always thrown at her. That not only was she barren but she was also dry as a desert.

She hadn't understood his accusation, but now she knew there wasn't anything wrong with her. She hadn't felt physical desire for her husband, and he hadn't concerned himself with her needs. But she did feel desire for Holbrook, and every part of her yearned for him to touch her however he wanted.

"If that is what you wish, my lord."

He released her and took two steps back. It was so sudden she almost stumbled.

"What I wish is to watch you undress."

His words, the heat in his eyes, his sensual demand… *Yes.* She would give this man everything if he continued to look at her as though she were the most desirable woman in the world.

She turned so her back was to him and looked at him over her shoulder. "I need help with the buttons. If I'd known you'd be ravishing me today, I would have worn something that was easier to remove."

His only reply was a deep, guttural groan that filled her with longing.

His hands made quick work of the small row of buttons at the back of her dress. When he parted the fabric, she didn't have to ask him to help her with her half corset. He undid the laces and then stepped away again to watch.

She stood with her back to him, her dress now gaping, but she was still watching him. She enjoyed the way his eyes were riveted on his handiwork. "You're quite good at that, my lord."

He met her gaze. "I have two rules before we continue. One, there will be no talk of other women when I'm here with you. There *are* no other women."

She shivered at his words. "And the second rule?"

"I have a name."

That he did. Mansfield had enjoyed her referring to him as her lord. She suspected it had to do with the fact she was the daughter of a duke and he a baron. It made him feel important.

But if there was to be no other women in this bedchamber, there would be no other men as well. From this point forward, she wouldn't think about what had transpired between her and her deceased husband.

"Yes, Holbrook."

He reached for her and spun her around so she faced him. She'd been holding her dress up, but the quick movement caused her to release her grip on the fabric. As though her garments were throwing themselves onto the floor before him, her dress and corset fell.

She was now standing before him in her chemise.

"Lucas. I only became Holbrook a few years ago."

She frowned. "Lucas and Lucy?"

Holbrook chuckled. "Yes, apparently we're a matched set. But no one other than my mother and brothers call me by my given name."

"Lucas." After her initial surprise at the similarity in their names, she decided she liked the way it sounded.

His gaze raked over her figure in a slow, leisurely perusal. She knew what he'd see. Her dusky nipples would be visible through the thin fabric of her white chemise. As would the dark triangle of hair between her thighs.

"All of it." The words were low, barely audible.

His eyes locked on hers, and she hesitated. Was she actually going to do this? She'd only ever been naked in front of her lady's maid when she was taking her bath, and even then Lucy usually moved quickly. She'd never stood bare in front of anyone and allowed them to examine her body.

But Holbrook had been staring at her for some time now, and her chemise was so thin she might as well be wearing nothing. Besides, she didn't want the type of romantic relationship she'd already experienced.

She lifted her hands and toyed with the small ribbon between her breasts that held the chemise in place. Holbrook's eyes were riveted on her hands, and a shiver went through her.

She wanted this as much as he did.

Slowly she pulled on the ribbon and loosened the small bow. The edges of fabric gaped open, showing the tops of her breasts.

With a small wiggle of her shoulders, she allowed the garment to fall to the floor. She was now standing completely naked amid the pile of her clothing.

Holbrook's—no, Lucas's—gaze took a leisurely path down her body again.

Her cheeks heated, and she could feel warmth spread throughout her. "Are you going to just stand there and stare at me?"

"If I had any talent, I would paint you like this. A wicked temptress trying to bring about my downfall."

There was no hint of lightness in his words, and she realized he was speaking the truth.

"I am infinitely thankful that you don't."

Finally he closed the space between them and

tugged her against his own fully clothed body. Sensations assailed her. Her heated skin touching the fine wool of his coat, her breasts pressed against the cool silk of his waistcoat. And beneath that, his hard body and arms surrounding her.

Never before had she found herself so desperate for a man's touch.

Her body yearned for the release he'd shown her with just his hands. And it had been far too long since he'd kissed her.

She tilted her chin up, and his mouth came down on hers as though they'd choreographed the movement. He devoured her with his kiss, and she returned it with equal passion.

She let out a small gasp and wrapped her arms around his neck when he tore his mouth away from hers and swept her into his arms. He carried her to the bed and then deposited her on it.

Now it was her turn to watch him disrobe. He shrugged out of his tailcoat and then undid the cravat that hid the column of his throat. Her eyes lingered on the broad width of the shoulders he'd just revealed and then fixed on his fingers as he deftly unbuttoned and removed his waistcoat. Finally he pulled his shirt up over his head.

He stood there, still wearing his trousers but bared to the waist.

Her mouth was dry as she took in his muscles. She'd known he was more muscular than her husband, but his clothing had hidden just how much.

She stretched her arm out to touch the only piece of bare skin within reach from her prone position on the bed. His abdomen.

He hissed out a breath as she ran her fingers over his skin. "You're so hard."

He closed his eyes tightly for a moment as though he were in pain. "You have no idea."

Her gaze moved down, and she saw the clear evidence of his arousal. But instead of freeing himself, he settled onto the bed next to her.

"I think you're wearing far too much clothing for what we need to do next."

One corner of his mouth quirked up. "I need to keep them on, temptress, if I'm to keep from ravaging you."

She frowned. "I hope you haven't changed your mind. I think I'd like to be ravaged."

He ran a large hand along her arm. "I want to explore you first. To taste you."

Shivers bloomed along her skin, and she didn't

have to wait long to learn what he meant. He kissed the side of her throat and then trailed a path downward.

She was shocked when the swipe of his tongue along her collarbone caused a shiver to go through her. She'd never known she could be so sensitive there. Of course he didn't stop, and before long he was nuzzling her breasts.

She ached with need but couldn't name what it was she wanted. Fortunately she didn't have to worry because Holbrook drew one nipple into his mouth and sucked. The pull of his mouth had her arching up into him. It also caused the ache between her legs to intensify.

She'd never imagined it would be possible for her to feel so wanton. So greedy for a man's touch.

After giving her other breast equal attention, He lifted his head and met her gaze. His eyes were dark with longing. "I'm going to taste all of you."

Her brows drew together. Wasn't he already doing that? But then he started dropping a line of kisses down to her belly, and she felt a hint of alarm as a truly wicked thought occurred to her.

No, surely he wasn't going to do *that*. Charlotte had told her that some men liked to pleasure a woman with their mouths, but she'd thought her friend was teasing her. She hadn't asked if her brother had ever done that to Charlotte because she really didn't want to know. There were some images she didn't need in her head.

Holbrook would never… He parted her legs and stared at her *there*, where no one had ever looked. Not even her husband.

Holbrook had already touched her there and brought her pleasure, but the fact that he was now looking at her wet folds was almost too much to bear.

She tried to push him away, but he didn't budge. "What are you doing?"

He met her gaze. "Do you trust me?"

She'd already told him that she did, but this was intimacy beyond anything she could have imagined. She was nervous but couldn't deny that a part of her yearned to experience everything he could show her.

She nodded and held her breath.

Only to feel it rushing out of her when he kissed her high on her inner thigh. And then he kissed her *there*.

She knew the pleasure he could give her with his fingers, but the heat of his mouth, the sounds he was making, as though he was enjoying doing this to her… Her mind blanked, and the entirety of the world existed only in the two of them in this bed. She could think of nothing except the feel of his mouth on her, doing wickedly delicious things she'd never imagined possible.

When he slipped two fingers inside her, her body tightened and then shuddered with release. She cried out, her hands fisting the bedding.

When she opened her eyes, he was on his knees over her, staring at her. "You're the most beautiful creature I've ever seen."

She shook her head, knowing that wasn't true. There were plenty of women more beautiful than her.

He rose from the bed, and she watched as his hands moved to his trousers, tracked the way his long, lean fingers worked at the fall. She'd already found release, but it seemed her body yearned for more.

He pushed his trousers down with impatience, and his manhood sprang free, long and hard.

She was unable to hold back a moan. His fingers within her had felt incredible filling her up, but she was afraid his length would tear her apart.

He was longer and thicker than she'd expected. "I don't know—"

He settled over her, his hard body covering her completely. But he held enough of his weight on his forearms that she wouldn't find it difficult to breathe.

She was very aware of the way his cock settled there, between her legs, and any reservation she might have had fled. In that moment she only knew that she needed Holbrook inside her right now.

"Please don't make me stop," he ground out.

The fact that he was still giving her the choice about whether to continue shattered the last of her doubts about this man.

She cupped his face in her hands and stared into his eyes. "Don't stop."

She made room for him between her thighs, and he pushed inside her with a groan. For a moment she feared he wouldn't fit, but her body opened, allowing him to sink into her all the way.

She was filled with awe. "You feel amazing."

"Not half as amazing as you, my love."

He began to move. Impossibly, her body seemed to grow even wetter with each thrust. She was already close to the edge, and it didn't take long for another orgasm to wash over her.

She'd never found release during lovemaking. She'd been half-afraid it wouldn't happen with

Holbrook now. Joy swamped through her as she clung to him, her legs and arms wrapping around him as she waited for him to find his own release.

She'd expected him to finish quickly, but he didn't. He kept going, thrusting into her with relentless strokes that seemed to demand everything from her.

Somehow her body tightened around him again, and she cried out his name. Only then, after her third release that day, did he push fully inside her and find his own pleasure.

CHAPTER 16

$\mathcal{H}$olbrook barely held back his curse. He'd meant to pull out before finding his release, but instead, he'd finished inside her like an untried youth.

He rolled them over, and she snuggled against him. He loved the way she curled into his chest like a tiny kitten seeking his warmth, but his satisfaction was marred by worry.

Despite being married for many years, she'd never conceived, but that didn't mean she never would. He ran a hand up and down her back as he imagined her belly round with his child. A different kind of longing settled somewhere in the vicinity of his heart.

He'd never given any thought to having children

aside from knowing it would happen at some point in the future. But now that future was in question because it was entirely possible Lucy wouldn't be able to give him an heir.

He tried to imagine giving her up. It was what she said she wanted from him—a love affair instead of courtship. That would free him to find someone else…

Panic seized him at the thought. No, he couldn't let her go. He had brothers. One of them could become the next viscount if he never fathered a son, because he wanted Lucy more than anyone—or anything—else. The viscountcy be damned.

Lucy raised her head, smiled, and cupped his cheek with one hand. "I can hear you thinking. Is something the matter? Did I do something wrong?"

He shifted so they were both on their sides, facing each other, and kissed her. "You, my temptress, are perfect."

"Tell me what's troubling you."

He blew out a breath. It seemed they were going to have this conversation now. "I was careless at the end."

A small vee formed between her brows. "Careless?"

"I finished inside you. I should have pulled out so as not to risk pregnancy."

Her eyes searched his for several seconds. Then she rolled onto her back and stared up at the ceiling. "I might be barren."

He leaned onto an elbow and looked down at her. "But you might not be. It is no secret that your husband had affairs. Did he father any children with those women?"

"None that I'm aware of." She sighed and covered her face with her hands.

He waited, watching her carefully to ensure he hadn't caused her any distress. One minute passed, and he could no longer stand her silence. If she was angry with him—either for being reckless or for mentioning her husband—he wanted her to let it out. He couldn't make things better if she didn't speak to him.

He pulled her hands away from her face. "Tell me what you're thinking. Yell at me if you must, but please don't shut me out."

She gave him a small smile. "I'm not upset, but I'm afraid you might be when I admit that I don't care if I fall pregnant. In fact, I'd consider it a blessing."

His heart soared at her words. "This isn't the

most romantic place to do this, but will you do me the honor—"

Her hands covered his mouth, and she shook her head. "No, no, no…"

His foolish hopes came crashing back to earth. He waited for her to remove her hands and then said, "One denial was sufficient."

She sat up and he did the same. He placed an arm around her shoulders and held her to his side, half-afraid she was going to flee.

She leaned into him and wrapped her arms around his waist. "It is now my turn to apologize." She gave a wry laugh. "I wasn't turning down your proposal. Well, not exactly. But I was horrified you might have thought I'd engineered things—telling you first that I wanted just an affair and then telling you I hoped I was pregnant—to force a marriage proposal from you."

The small flicker of hope reignited in his chest. "So you're saying you *will* accept my proposal?"

She crawled onto his lap, straddling him, and he was powerless to stem his renewed desire for her. "I am saying that I will consider it."

He didn't think he'd ever smiled so widely in his life. But he couldn't find it within him to care if he looked foolish.

He brought her hips closer so her core was flush against his cock. "Is there anything I can do to sway your decision?"

She shifted her hips against him, dragging her wet folds over his hardness with a soft murmur of approval. "I am always willing to consider a logical argument— Oh!" Her breath shattered on the last word as he lifted her and rammed her down onto him. "And I must say, you do seem to have a very persuasive way about you."

He laughed, allowing hope to bubble through him. She was going to be his—he could feel it in his bones. Lucy was still holding on to her stubbornness, but he'd wait for her however long it took. Until then, he was going to do everything in his power to see that she became addicted to his touch.

"You've created a monster, Lucy. Now that I've given into temptation, you're never going to get rid of me."

Her arms tightened around his shoulders, and she leaned into him, taking over, her body rising and falling over his. She spoke softly against his mouth. "That might not be such a bad thing."

There was no longer any need to hold back, and he gave himself over completely, without guilt, to his desire.

Lucy was thinking about accepting his proposal. She *wanted* to have a child with him, so there was no need to take precautions.

Now he just had to figure out how to spend more time with her because he doubted Clarington would allow him unfettered access to his sister's body.

He'd need to count on the assistance of allies who were rooting for them, chief among them the duchess.

But for now he would think only of the beautiful, vivacious woman in his arms. Her body tightened around him all too soon, and he couldn't hold back his own release.

She let out a soft moan and then a louder one while her orgasm went on and on. He held her in place as he followed, giving her every part of himself, body and soul.

Before too much longer, he vowed to make Lucy Mansfield the new Viscountess Holbrook.

CHAPTER 17

It was official. Every single one of Lucy's friends seemed intent on seeing a match made between her and Holbrook. Over the next few weeks, they were paired up at a surprising number of private dinner parties. And if Lucy visited Hatchard's bookshop with Lady Hargrove, she discovered that Holbrook was already there with her friend's husband.

The second time it happened, she realized it wasn't a coincidence. For a moment she'd suspected Holbrook had engineered the meeting, but the exasperated huff he'd aimed at Lord Hargrove, followed by the earl's grin, told her he'd been just as surprised.

During larger social events, Holbrook took care to remain close by. They weren't betrothed, so it would cause a stir if he remained by her side the entire evening, but it was clear that was what he wanted.

And heaven help her, so did she.

If she had any lingering doubts about Holbrook's character as the season progressed, they'd been thoroughly erased. And yet she still had one fear that was impossible to banish.

Every Wednesday, Holbrook called to take her to Hyde Park, but instead, he brought her to his town house. He'd shown her exactly why her friends were so happily married. Why they didn't dread their husband's touch as Lucy had dreaded Mansfield's visits when he'd still bothered.

During their all-too-brief moments together, she'd come to a horrible realization. She loved Holbrook. He was in her heart more deeply than Mansfield had ever been.

Which was why that Wednesday, when he brought them to his town house, she didn't immediately fly into his arms the moment the bedroom door was closed.

He lifted one brow. "Is something the matter?"

She'd thought this moment would be difficult. To her surprise, it was the opposite. But then everything with Holbrook felt natural and easy. And she knew, without a doubt, that he would do anything for her.

Which was why she needed to give him the chance to back away now if he had even the smallest doubt about their future.

"The season will be coming to an end soon."

He stared at her for several seconds before finally speaking. "Is it just the season that is ending?"

His jaw was tense, his stare solemn, and she realized what he must be thinking. That she was seeking to put an end to their affair.

She closed the space between them and cradled his face in her hands. "No, that wasn't what I was saying."

He closed his eyes, and she felt the shudder that ran through his body before he held her close to his heart.

She'd bungled this badly. When he pulled away again, she smiled at him. "I only meant to say that we need to decide what will happen next. My brother is returning to his country seat, but I have nowhere else I need to be. I can stay in London."

He took hold of her hands and brought them together, holding them against his chest. Against his heart. She could feel the strong, steady thrum of its beat through their clasped hands.

"I need to return to the country, Lucy. My mother plans to visit."

A shard of ice pierced her heart. Holbrook was leaving?

Her initial instinct was to pull away. Tell him goodbye, perhaps offer one more afternoon together. And then she'd escape and hide away in her bedchamber at her brother's town house.

She didn't know where the instinct came from, but a wave of denial flowed through her. It was so powerful she almost didn't recognize her voice when she spoke. "No. You can't leave."

"Come with me, Lucy. Marry me. I can get a special license and we can be married before the end of the season."

She hesitated.

"I love you, Lucy. I'll wait for you. And if this is all I can ever have with you, then it will be enough. I'll return to London as soon as I'm able, and we can spend as much time together as we want."

The words burst out of her. "What if I can't give you children? You'll come to hate me." It was her worst fear. That she would be a disappointment to him. She didn't worry that he would turn away from her as her husband had done, but that didn't mean she wanted to be a burden to him.

He shook her gently. "The last time I checked, there was no way for any woman to know whether she'd be able to carry a child. Yet people get married all the time."

She smiled, touched by his desire to comfort her. "And husbands then grow to resent their barren wives."

"Not all of them. I wouldn't. All I want is you."

"But—"

"Lucy, I have three brothers. I don't *need* an heir. I already have a handful of them. Would I like a child? I'm not going to lie and say I wouldn't dote on a little girl who looked just like her beautiful mother. Although I suppose I'd also love her if she looked more like me."

The wry twist of his lips startled a surprised laugh out of her. She threw her arms around him, too overcome with emotion to speak.

To his credit, he simply held her and waited. Ever patient. *Hers.*

When she pulled back, he lifted a hand to brush away the tears that were silently sliding down her cheeks. "Are these happy tears or sad tears?"

"They're happy tears," she managed with a broken sob. "I love you so much."

"Does that mean you'll marry me?"

"Yes, Lucas. It was always going to be yes."

He brushed his mouth over hers. "I'll spend every day of my life trying to be worthy of you."

"You already are," she whispered against his mouth before deepening the kiss. Then she proceeded to show him just how much she loved him.

EPILOGUE #1

A LETTER FROM HOLBROOK'S MOTHER

Lucas,

I was very pleased to receive your letter informing us of your upcoming nuptials at the end of the season... Which, good heavens, is almost upon us!

You might have prepared me sooner. I had no notion you were looking for a bride this year. I would have happily joined you in London to offer my assistance. You know how much I prefer the country, but for my beloved firstborn, I would have made the sacrifice.

I will be departing as soon as possible.

And since your brothers are newly arrived home from Eton, they'll be joining me. Pray that I survive the trip down. You cannot imagine what a trial it is sharing a carriage with those three boys.

The house is in an uproar as we make the preparations. You should know that your brothers are already making plans to turn London upside down. I will have to rely on you to help me with them.

With much love and kisses from your devoted mother.
XXXXX

Postscript—If I make the trip all the way to London only to learn you've already married by special license, I will be most aggrieved.

EPILOGUE #2

August 1819

Clarington Estate, Kent

Sitting on the edge of a picnic blanket, Lucy basked in the bucolic scene that surrounded her. She loved visiting her brother's estate, and it had been far too many years since she'd been able to visit the house in which she'd grown up.

She smiled. Watching the children play and run around brought back happy memories of her own childhood, playing on these very grounds. But today there were decidedly more children. All her brother's friends and their families were visiting, and the estate was filled with laughing children. Some were giving chase, but she didn't miss the small group of girls who were off to one side. They were whispering to each other and giggling while they cast what they thought were surreptitious glances at another group of boys. They'd find out soon enough what the girls were planning. That was the good thing about children. They couldn't hold back their secrets for long.

Their parents had all paired up and were strolling through the grounds. They took turns standing on the opposite side of the open area in which the picnic had been set up to ensure none of the children wandered too far afield.

Lucy remembered well the panic she'd felt when she'd snuck into the maze when no one was watching and then been unable to find her way out. Alex had found her an hour later, hopelessly lost and crying.

Feeling eyes on her, she glanced over to the opening of that maze and found her brother standing there, barring the entrance. And she had the uncanny thought that he was remembering that exact same moment.

Holbrook joined her on the picnic blanket then. He dropped into position behind her, his long legs stretched out on either side. She leaned back into him, enjoying the way he surrounded her. The feel of his hard body, his scent filling her nostrils, never failed to soothe her.

He placed his hands over her still-flat belly. "How are you and the little one, my love?"

She sighed and closed her eyes. "Exhausted. Charlotte warned me I'd be tired during the beginning months, but I never imagined I'd be *this* tired."

He dropped a kiss on top of her head, and she hummed with pleasure. She could fall asleep just like this.

After a minute Holbrook spoke. "I never expected I could be so happy."

Joy blossomed in her chest. Neither had she. But with Holbrook, safely held in his arms and carrying their child… "I never imagined I could have everything I've ever dreamed of. But you've made that possible."

She turned to look at him, and he dropped a kiss onto her lips. "We've made that possible together."

Clarington stood in place at the entrance to the maze. Today was a happy day, and he didn't want anyone wandering into the maze and getting lost. Soon enough he'd ask a footman to take over the duty, but for now he enjoyed standing back and taking in the happy scene before him. Out of the corner of his eye, he saw his wife sweep into the middle of the open area and knew she'd be collecting children for their game of pall-mall.

His gaze met Lucy's, and a quiet moment of understanding passed between them. She was remembering that day as well. It was an unsettling thought that he'd allowed her to be lost and unhappy for far too many years, but she'd finally found her way out of the tangled maze of despair her life had been.

Holbrook joined her, and Clarington watched them together. Lucy's eyes were closed, and she rested against his chest. Holbrook held her as though she was the most precious object in the world.

He heard footsteps approach, but he didn't have to turn to see who it was.

The Earl of Brantford stopped and stood next to him. Together, they watched Lucy and Holbrook.

After a minute, Brantford spoke. "The outcome was satisfactory."

"Yes," Clarington said. "I knew she'd come through the scandal." He'd had some help with that, too, from Brantford. The man was no longer referred to as the Unaffected Earl, but he still commanded a surprising amount of power and influence.

"I regret that it took so long," Brantford said. "For all his vices, the man didn't sleep with that many married women."

Of course not. Lucy's first husband had always had an uncanny knack for self-preservation. But in the end, he'd finally bedded the wrong woman. And

Brantford had whispered a few words in the right ears, guaranteeing that Mansfield be called out.

He turned to face the earl. "I am in your debt. If there's ever anything I can do for you, you need only ask."

Brantford's expression didn't change, but Clarington thought he detected a hint of warmth enter the man's eyes. "It is a pleasure seeing your sister happy. But since I have your attention… tell me what you know about the Legends."

EPILOGUE #4

THE MAYFAIR CHRONICLE

April 1820

I'm sure there are quite a few gentlemen who will be aggrieved to learn that Lady Holbrook (formerly the widowed Baroness Mansfield, sister to the powerful Duke of Clarington) has given birth to twins.

The accomplished and beautiful viscountess has seen fit to carry both a boy, providing her husband with an heir, and a girl. (There is nothing more tragic than a second son who missed being an heir by a matter of minutes…)

Our felicitations go out to Viscount Holbrook and Lady Holbrook.

And to all those men who engaged in the vile bet to make the woman their mistress, this author has it on good authority that the viscountess's brother has discovered their identities…

But I know many of you are here for more salacious news.

This author has recently heard a particularly tasty rumor about a certain lord who has become legendary…

I loved having the opportunity to come full circle with this series. *Dancing with the Duke* was an introductory novella to my *Landing a Lord* series. It begins with Clarington, who was dragged to Almack's by his mother and sister. I loved the symmetry of giving him the final scene in this series as well.

The *Landing a Lord* series was originally conceived as a three-book series about the Evans family—Louisa, Catherine, and John. Along the way other characters showed up who demanded their own stories be told.

I hope you enjoyed the Easter egg reference about Brantford's wife and sister giving self-defence lessons to women. It's something I always thought they would do, and I'm glad I was able to share that piece of their story with you.

If you're curious about the Legends, sign up for my newsletter on suzannamedeiros.com to be among the first to learn more about their books when they're available.

Holbrook's mother signs her letter with a row of Xs. The first definitive use of this symbol to denote kisses was in Florence Montgomery's 1878 book *Seaforth*. But there is some debate as to whether a 1763 letter from Gil White, which was signed with a row of Xs, was used to denote kisses or blessings. Both can apply here so I took the liberty.

TURN THE PAGE FOR AN EXCERPT FROM *A ROGUE for Christmas*, which is book 3 in my CHRISTMAS SCANDALS series…

If he was a better man, he'd stay far away from Iris
Rowland. But no one had ever accused the Earl of
Wentworth of being a good man.

After saving Iris from certain ruin the unthinkable
happens. He becomes obsessed with the memory of
the young woman he rescued at the end of the
season.

There is only one thing to do. Secure an invitation
to the Christmas house party she'll be attending.
But instead of putting his curiosity about Iris to rest,
he is shocked to discover that his inconvenient
attraction might be something more.

If he were a better man, he'd stay far away from Miss Iris Rowland. But no one had ever accused the Earl of Wentworth of being a good man. Which was why he'd gone out of his way to secure an invitation to Viscount Thornton's annual Christmas house party.

It was a calculated risk since he couldn't be certain Iris would be in attendance. But his discreet inquiries had shown this was his best course of action. His only path forward, really, if he didn't want to wait until the next season began before he could see her again.

It had been years since Wentworth had ventured into the country for Christmas. Normally he spent the day in London, where he wouldn't have to listen to his mother's constant lectures about his unbecoming conduct. Staying in town also made it easier to conduct his affairs.

Not that he'd engaged in any liaisons of late, which was precisely the reason he was in Surrey. Iris Rowland was constantly in his thoughts—he'd even dreamed about her. Drastic action was needed to exorcise whatever spell she'd cast over him.

He'd only spoken to her once, and their

encounter had been brief, but every second of their meeting out in the gardens during the last ball of the season was etched in his memory.

He'd grown bored early in the evening and made arrangements to meet an overeager new widow for a bit of fun. He'd been finding it increasingly difficult to enjoy his customary amusements of late and feared he was growing jaded. Hoping it was only a phase, he slipped out into the dimly lit gardens.

The moon wasn't positioned correctly to supply enough light that evening, and the large shrubs and flowering bushes cast dark shadows along the path. But light wasn't a requirement for what would happen tonight. One body was very much like another in the dark.

He blamed the shadows for his error in mistaking the woman standing in the garden for the buxom widow.

She was already waiting for him, facing away. He let out a sigh as he moved into place behind her. She was too old to make the mistake of turning her back on the path, where anyone could come across her.

He placed his arms on her hips and dragged her back into him. His mouth was already dropping to the exposed expanse of skin at the base of her neck when the unexpected happened. She raised her arm, but instead of reaching back to bury her fingers in his hair, she brought her elbow back sharply against his midsection.

It wasn't enough to hurt him, of course, but he released her at once. He enjoyed his dalliances, but he would never force a woman. Seduce her, yes, but he'd never use force. He was also annoyed that she was playing games with him. If this woman thought that he was going to chase her to get what he wanted, she would be sorely disappointed.

He was preparing to tell her just that as she spun around to face him, but the admonition died on his lips.

Dammit, this wasn't the eager widow from the ballroom. No, the indignant young woman was the last person he'd expected to find here.

Iris Rowland. Sister-in-law to the Earl of Seaford and, from all indications, an innocent.

He watched the play of emotions cross her lovely face. Indignation, then shock. Her blue eyes widened, and her hands flew to her lips. Her cheeks were red, but he watched the color fade within moments.

"Oh! You're not—"

She seemed to think better of revealing who she'd planned to meet and snapped her lips closed.

"I take it you were expecting someone else?"

He thought she'd shake her head in denial. Perhaps babble some excuse and then flee. Instead, she folded her arms at her waist and frowned at him. The position framed her bodice, and he was powerless to stop his gaze from lowering to her breasts. Her bounty was more modest than the widow, but he found himself wondering how it would feel to drag this woman into his arms and make love to her.

"Are you quite done?"

He laughed. "You can cease playing the scandalized maiden, Miss Rowland. We both know why you are out here in the gardens late at night."

Her mouth dropped open, and then she glared at him. Actually glared. It was an amusing change of pace. Normally, women went out of their way to make themselves attractive—and available—to him. And young women newly out in society, well, they avoided him altogether.

But it seemed that Miss Rowland was made of sterner stuff. To his absolute shock, he was intrigued.

"You might be out here for other… nefarious reasons. But I just wanted to enjoy the gardens."

He crossed his arms, mimicking her stance, and held her gaze for several seconds. She looked away first.

She'd been angry that he'd dragged her against him, so perhaps she was telling the truth and thought that a man would meet her here late at night, alone, and not want to touch her.

"Who did you think I was when you spun around?"

Her lips firmed into a tight line, and he wanted to shake her. Surely her family didn't know she was sneaking out into the gardens to take in the flowers with some bloke who would think nothing of ruining her.

"You need to stay away from the gardens at night. They're frequented by rogues and ne'er-do-wells."

She lifted her chin, which somehow, despite the fact that he was at least a foot taller than her, had the effect of making it appear as though she were looking down at him. "Perhaps that was what I was seeking? Someone who wasn't tame."

He was fairly certain her demeanor was a show of bravado. Clearly Miss Rowland needed someone to shake her out of her complacency. To show her that the world wasn't a safe place for gently bred young women.

He moved closer, aware of the way she drew him to her like a magnet. Normally he'd be putting as much space as possible between himself and someone who was fresh on the marriage mart.

"Are you looking for danger, Miss Rowland?"

©2023 Suzanna Medeiros

BOOKS BY SUZANNA MEDEIROS

Dear Stranger

Forbidden in February

Anthologies:

The Novellas: A Collection

Hathaway Heirs: Books 1-4

Landing a Lord: Books 1-3

Landing a Lord: Books 4-6

Landing a Lord series:

Dancing with the Duke

Loving the Marquess

Beguiling the Earl

The Unaffected Earl

The Unsuitable Duke

The Unexpected Marquess

The Unwilling Viscount

The Baron's Return

Courting the Earl

Tempting the Viscount

Christmas Scandals series:

A Viscount for Christmas

A Highwayman for Christmas

A Rogue for Christmas

Hathaway Heirs series:

Lady Hathaway's Proposal

Lord Hathaway's Bride

Captain Hathaway's Dilemma

Miss Hathaway's Wish

For more information and an up-to-date booklist please visit the author's website:

www.suzannamedeiros.com/books/

ABOUT SUZANNA

USA Today bestselling author Suzanna Medeiros was born and raised in Toronto, Canada. Her love for the written word led her to pursue a degree in English Literature from the University of Toronto. She went on to earn a Bachelor of Education degree but graduated at a time when no teaching jobs were available. After working at a number of interesting places, including a federal inquiry, a youth probation office, and the Office of the Fire Marshal of Ontario, she decided to pursue her first love—writing.

Suzanna is married to her own hero and survived raising twins. She is an avowed romantic who enjoys spending her days writing love stories.

She would like to thank her parents for showing her that love at first sight and happily ever after really do exist.

To learn about Suzanna Medeiros's future books
sign up for her newsletter:
https://www.suzannamedeiros.com/newsletter

Visit her website:
https://www.suzannamedeiros.com

Or visit her on Facebook:
https://www.facebook.com/AuthorSuzanna
Medeiros

9 781988 223605